Hero De Jure

The Justice Thalia Stories
Snowfall
Murder Most Fowl

888-555-HERO
Hero De Facto
Hero Ad Hoc
Hero De Novo
A Very Hero Christmas
Hero De Jure
Hero In Camera
Hero Amicus Curiae (Coming Soon)
A Very Hero Wedding (Coming Soon)
Hero Ad Litem (Coming Soon)

Millersburg Magick Mysteries
Spells and Sleuths
Fae and Felonies
Magick and Murder

Miscellaneous
Sword and Sorceress 31 ("Pig-Headed")
Sword and Sorceress 32 ("Unexpected")

For updates, news, and giveaways, join Suzan's mailing list or visit her website at www.suzanharden.com. You can also check her out on Twitter or Facebook.

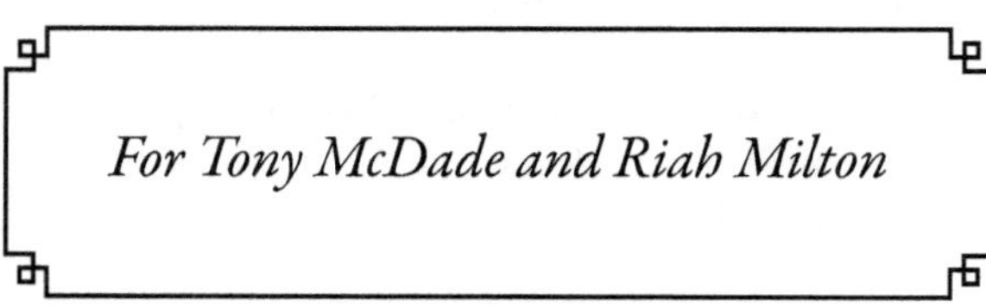

HERO DE JURE (888-555-HERO #5)
Copyright 2020 by Suzan Harden
All rights reserved
ISBN-13 - 978-1-938745-74-4

Published by Angry Sheep Publishing
Findlay, Ohio

Interior Design by QA Productions
Cover Design by For the Muse Designs

Hero De Jure

888-555-HERO #5

Suzan Harden

CHAPTER 1

"Harri!"

Patty Ames's shriek preceded her bursting through Harri Winters' office door, her blond curls bouncing in her wake. "You've got to see this!" She rushed to Harri's secondhand maple desk and grabbed the TV remote, her pale face even whiter than usual.

The Action 12! News logo flashed in the bottom right corner of the supersize screen hanging on the wall opposite from Harri's desk. But it wasn't Canyon Pointe's skyline in the video.

Instead, a panoramic view of San Francisco Bay and the Golden Gate Bridge filled the screen. The bridge glowed under the rising sun.

Until a dark blur hit the north end of the city's famous landmark.

Cables snapped and flailed. Bits and pieces fell, but from the distant perspective, they were probably slabs of pavement and chunks of metal larger than Harri's ancient Honda. Vehicles tumbled hundreds of feet into the vicious bay current. Harri covered her mouth with her hand to keep from screaming as well. They were watching innocent commuters plunging to their deaths. Even if every super in California and the surrounding states had been there, they couldn't have saved everyone.

Aisha, Susan, and Arthur darted into Harri's office and stared at the TV screen, no doubt their attention drawn by Patty's shriek.

"... current death toll is unknown. The damage to the San Francisco icon allegedly happened during a battle between Ultramegaperson and Doctor Liquidation that started at the San Francisco Federal Reserve." The camera shot switched to Action 12!'s evening co-anchor Essie Morales in the studio. This level of carnage required someone with poise, which Essie had in spades.

The analytical part of Harri wondered if Essie had beaten her co-anchor Ted Meadowfield to the studio, or if their producer Nella Lopez hadn't bothered to call him this morning. Ted never quite grasped the necessity of simply being polite to his co-workers.

Essie's concerned-journalist expression was firmly fixed on her beautiful face. As fixed as her black hair by styling products. "Ultramegaperson is assisting the Coast Guard in rescue efforts. Guy Montana, spokesman for the National Superhero Bureau, says a thorough investigation will be undertaken once all victims have been retrieved.

"Victims retrieved" was reporter-speak for the body recovery for an obscene number of deaths.

Essie's voice droned. "In other news, the Dow Jones—"

Patty hit the mute button and set the remote back on Harri's desk. "You want me to call them?"

Harri wearily shook her head at Patty's reference to the NSB. "No. Ultramegaperson will call us when they're able. No comment until we decide how we need to spin this."

The law firm's assistant nodded. Before she could take a step, the phone lines at her desk out in the reception area started buzzing. Patty rolled her eyes.

"What a way to start a Monday morning." She strode out of Harri's office.

"Arthur—" Harri started.

"On it. I'll see what I can retrieve." Arthur Drallhickey, the firm's head of IT and a reformed supervillain himself, charged out the office door. If anyone could dig through the bureaucratic bullshit and learn the truth, it was him. Harri ignored the fact that some of his techniques weren't exactly ethical. Or legal. But they needed as much information as they could get about the incident, especially since one of their top clients was involved in this mess.

"You two have any bright ideas?" Harri leaned her right elbow on the desktop, set her chin on her palm, and stared at her legal partners.

Aisha Franklin shook her head. Her hair no longer flipped all over the place. She had their closest friend Jeremy slice off her dreads not long after she delivered her first-born. Baby Mitch had a tendency to yank on them.

Hard enough she feared baldness. However, she pulled off the super-short, henna'd minifro Jeremy had styled like a supermodel.

"We need more information first." Aisha gestured toward the TV screen which was replaying the top news story after Essie's brief update on other headlines. "What hit the bridge?"

"Considering its size, it wasn't a person." Susan Kennedy pushed a lock of her red hair behind her ear while she watched the replay closely. Harri had originally hired their former law school classmate nearly a year ago to cover for Aisha during maternity leave. Susan had an excellent legal mind, a ton of trial experience, and was pretty damn patient considering the chaos Harri and Aisha's personal lives had been during the initial months Susan was with them. That patience made her a good fit for the firm.

Out in the reception area, Harri could hear Patty repeating, "No comment," like it was a Buddhist mantra.

Aisha stalked over to Harri's office door and closed it. "Now's when I really wish I could drink coffee again."

"Wean Mitch early." Harri grinned at her partner.

"Your godson's only four months old." Aisha gave her a dirty look. "He's not even eating solids yet."

"But is he flying?" Harri continued to tease.

If Aisha had laser vision in her superpower arsenal, Harri would have been a crispy critter.

"When you two are finished bickering—" Susan started to say, but Harri's intercom buzzed, interrupting her.

Patty wouldn't interrupt them unless this was super important.

Harri poked the appropriate button on her phone set. "Yes?"

"Nella is on line one," Patty chirped.

"I'll handle Nella. Transfer her to my phone, Patty." Aisha strode toward Harri's office door. "Find out what hit the Golden Gate, and you'd better hope it wasn't something our client actually did." She left, closing the door once again.

No doubt Nella Lopez, Action 12! News's senior producer, was hoping to finagle an exclusive out of Aisha. Harri would be the first to admit her best friend was better at handling the publicity side of their boutique clientele.

"She's right." Susan snatched the remote and thumbed the slow-motion button as Action 12! News began to replay their film of the morning's incident for the fourth time.

Ultramegaperson could be the biggest twat waffle on the planet at times, but they had come through when Aisha needed some help last Christmas. And the fees from the trans superhero alone kept the firm afloat this year.

That money was a godsend. Aisha had wanted a careful well-thought-out plan to introduce hers and her husband Rey Garcia's new superhero identities. She had also wanted to shed the baby weight before she squeezed into spandex again.

Harri couldn't blame Aisha for that. Spandex showed everything.

However, the care was necessary. The rush job they'd done with Rey's first persona, Captain Justice, had blown up in their faces thanks to the supervillain Professor Paranoia. The saving grace was they knew Paranoia was roasting in a top security prison in Japan.

The intercom buzzed again, and Harri tapped the button. "Yeah, Patty?"

"Ultramegaperson is on line two."

Harri hit the speaker function. "Hey, Ultra! We saw the news. Susan's here with me. What do you need from us?"

"Um, Harri," the superhero said hesitantly. "I'm under arrest."

CHAPTER 2

Aisha grabbed the receiver from her phone set, hit the button beside the flashing light, and leaned back in her chair. "Hi, Nella! What can I do for you?"

"Is Winters & Franklin going to issue a statement about Ultramegaperson's arrest?" the producer blurted.

Shock ran through Aisha. She concentrated a bit. With her enhanced hearing, she could tell Harri was on the phone with their client. Part of her had been upset to know what she thought had been HRSP, as hormone-related superpowers were known colloquially in pregnant women, wasn't going away after her son Mitch's birth. But sometimes, her new abilities came in handy.

"We can't comment on the alleged arrest at this time," Aisha said. "Not until we have a chance to talk to our client."

"You didn't know, did you?" Nella accused.

"Sorry, Nella, you know I can't officially answer that."

"But off the record?" the producer prompted.

"Would you want me telling your secrets?"

"Come on, Aisha." Nella's tone was somewhere between wheedling and threatening. "You don't want other people controlling your client's story."

Aisha rolled her eyes, even though Nella couldn't see the expression. "Is that your way of saying you're going to sic Ted on us if I don't say something now?" Ted Meadowfield, Essie's co-anchor, would literally sell his own mother for ratings. Especially after he lost out on a chance at an on-air reporting job at CBS. Calling the president of the news division's wife a bitch he'd like to tap in front of said president hadn't won him any admirers.

And Ted hated Harri with a passion matched only by the members of Corvus, a black-ops group who had been illegally recruiting supers and repeatedly tried to kill Harri until they were busted for attempting to assassinate a judge.

"It'll be harder for me to keep Ted on a leash if you don't give Essie something to use," Nella said.

"Blackmailer." Aisha knew there was a symbiotic relationship between the news makers and the news reporters. It didn't mean she liked it. She considered what spin to use. "We just received the official notice a few minutes before you called. I haven't talked with the San Francisco D.A.'s office or the Justice Department yet to find out what the specific charges are."

Well, that part was technically true. Aisha glanced at her computer screen for the current time. "Give me until three. Essie will have an exclusive statement for tonight's prime time broadcast."

"Deal!" Nella's voice was a little too gleeful. "But if you're a minute late, I'm going to have to run with what Ted learned."

Aisha's heart pounded. "What are you talking about?"

"Maybe you should talk to your client first." Nella's switch to reluctance in her attitude set off alarms in Aisha's brain.

"I'm not going to hang a client out to dry if you're planning to boil them anyway," Aisha bit out. "Spill."

"The governor of California and his security team were on the Golden Gate when it was hit."

Aisha fell back in her chair and struggled to breathe. "Is this confirmed?"

"Yeah," Nella said softly. "The web cameras on the bridge caught the governor's cortege falling. Our direct source has a close-up from a personal drone camera."

"May I please have a copy of the drone footage?"

The news producer hesitated a moment. "Our source didn't want to be named."

"I understand wanting to protect your sources, Nella," Aisha said gently. "But this source may have information as to who's really at fault here."

"You sure you're not just covering your bottom line?"

"Frankly, that would be a certain partner of mine's chief concern, but I left Dewey & Cheatham because they didn't give a rat's ass about the people underneath the masks or the civilians caught in the crossfire during these battles." Aisha waited a beat before she added, "Whoever was behind the Golden Gate Bridge incident needs to pay for what they've done."

"All right," Nella finally said. "But you don't get the footage until I get a statement."

"Agreed. Thanks for telling me about the video." Aisha swallowed hard. "I'll talk to you before three." She tapped the button to end the call and buried her face in her hands.

Oh, god. Ultramegaperson was so fucked.

CHAPTER 3

Harri swallowed hard as Susan's eyes met hers. "What are the charges, Ultra?"

"Multiple counts of second-degree murder." Ultramegaperson sounded like they were on the verge of tears. "That's just the beginning of the list. I won't know until they recover all the bodies. Harri, they won't even let me help with the-the-the—"

As much as Harri wanted to curl up in a ball at the horrible scene still replaying on her big screen, she needed to pull up her big girl panties and take care of business.

"Ultra, listen to me," Harri said. "Cooperate with the police as far as booking and holding. However—" Her voice deepened. "—under no circumstances do you say a word until I get there. Do you understand? Not a word."

"I-I—" The sound of Ultramegaperson taking a deep breath and releasing it whistled through the speaker. "I got it. Not a word until you get here."

"I'll be on the next flight," Harri reassured her client. "Hang in there, Ultra. We'll get this sorted out."

"Thanks, Harri." They hesitated a moment before the superhero added, "Can you call my emergency contact and tell them the same thing you told me?"

"Absolutely," Harri affirmed.

"Thank you," Ultramegaperson said again.

Once they ended the call, Susan blurted, "Ultra doesn't sound good."

"Would you?" Harri shook her head. "Even if the prosecutor pleads down to manslaughter, they're looking at spending the rest of their life in prison."

She reached for the remote and turned off the TV. "We're going to need local counsel. You know anyone in the Bay area you trust?"

Susan nodded. "I've worked with Gil Wilcrest a couple of times. He needs to retire, but he knows his supers law inside and out."

Worry niggled though Harri's brain. "What do you mean 'he needs to retire'?"

"He's eighty-nine." Susan grinned. "But you're not going to find anyone sharper."

"Wait a minute." Harri's coffee burbled in her stomach as Susan's original statement caught up to the hamster attempting to jumpstart her mind on a Monday morning. "Are you talking about Gilbert Amadeus Wilcrest? The person who practically wrote most of the supers' laws in the country? The only person to turn down a seat on the United States Supreme Court?"

"Yep." Susan nodded sharply. "Want me to give him a call?"

"Hell, yes!" Harri gestured affirmatively. "We'll pay him whatever the hell he wants as long as it doesn't involve first-born babies."

Susan grinned and strode to Harri's office door. She opened it, but before she could take a step outside, Aisha burst through the opening.

At superspeed.

She was exceptionally careful about displaying her powers, especially after she accidentally destroyed her kitchen table during a Braxton-Hicks contraction. Harri still didn't believe the damage to Aisha's refrigerator was an accident though.

"We've got a bigger problem than we thought," Aisha said. "The governor of California may have been killed in this morning's incident."

"May have been?" Harri exclaimed.

"He is, uh, was up for re-election." Anger glittered in Aisha's dark brown eyes. "There was a rally scheduled for this morning to be followed by a fundraising lunch. His escort was on the Golden Gate when it was struck. Nella says they have footage from one of the web cameras on the bridge showing the governor's motorcade going into the bay."

"Oh, my god!" All blood drained from Susan's face.

"It gets worse," Aisha said grimly. "A civilian with a drone got a close up shot of the vehicles going into the water."

"We've got to get that video—" Susan started.

"Wait a minute." Harri leaned back in her office chair. Something did not smell right. "Why was a civilian flying a drone that close to a national monument?"

"A good question." Aisha shrugged. "It's one I can't answer. Nella won't give me the video or the source's contact information until I give her an official statement."

"We've got another problem." Harri filled her partner in on Ultramegaperson's call.

"Shit." Aisha scrubbed her hands over her face. Her designer stilettos left the carpet and she floated up a good six inches.

"Girl, I do not have the time or the patience to pry you off the ceiling this morning," Harri snapped and pointed at her open blinds.

"Sorry." Aisha screwed up her face in concentration. She drifted back to the floor.

"If we don't stop that video from being released, Aisha floating through the office will be the least of our problems," Susan pointed out.

"It's already at the Channel 12's studio." Aisha planted her hands on her hips. "I'm not wasting my time or our client's money arguing a First Amendment issue that we *will* lose."

Harri tapped her pen against the yellow legal pad she'd been using for her to-do list. "What if this isn't a simple negligence issue?"

"What do you mean?" Susan asked.

But Aisha narrowed her eyes. "You really think Trubble is operating from prison?"

The frisson of worry worming inside Harri transformed into full-blown dread. If Aisha wasn't questioning Harri's harebrained suspicion, maybe they were in bigger trouble than she thought.

"Our newest client is about to be accused of assassinating the governor of California." Harri shrugged. "It's small potatoes compared to some of the stuff Black Death has done for them. Doctor Liquidation was recently released from prison on a technicality, but all her assets are still under federal control with the ongoing civil litigation. She'd be desperate for the cash. Pick a fight with Ultra. Spend thirty days in jail for civil disturbance. She thinks she'll be able to take the payoff and disappear to Mal Paraíso. No extradition. No way for anyone to grab whatever assets she has stashed there."

"Meanwhile, Ultramegaperson is stuck in the U.S., facing the fallout." Susan waved her right hand. "There doesn't need to be a conspiracy or a payoff to Doctor Liquidation for that to happen."

"Except Ultramegaperson just became our client five months ago," Aisha said sourly.

"Do you two realize how paranoid you sound?" Susan stared at Aisha and then Harri.

"It's not paranoia if they're really out to get you," Harri said wryly.

Arthur poked his huge schnoz around the edge of her office door and knocked on the doorjamb. "May I interrupt for a moment?"

"Come on in." Harri motioned for him to enter.

He looked at Aisha. "You were right. Nella has already made three copies of the video. She was making a fourth copy when I—"

Susan stuck her index fingers in her ears and started yelling, "La-la-la-la-la-la!"

Arthur glared at the newest partner with more than a trace of annoyance on his pasty features. He'd come a long way over the past year from the quivering supervillain wannabe to a valued member of their team.

Susan paused and carefully removed her fingers. "What have I said about telling me about the illegal shit you do?"

"Which is why only Harri and Aisha have copies to review on their laptops." The sad part of his statement was the total lack of snideness in his tone.

Aisha chuckled. "If Nella didn't want me to have the clip, she wouldn't have told me about it."

Harri leaned forward and tapped a key to close the screen saver while Susan started another round of la-la-la-la-ing. Sure enough, Arthur had already opened a window with the video primed. Harri tapped the play button.

Her partners gathered around her chair. She had the sensation of flying above vehicles as they approached the north end of the bridge. Ahead of the camera, she spotted a highway patrol cruiser leading three gray hybrid SUVs. Two CHP motorcycles tailed the group. All of the SUVs were flying mini U.S. and State of California flags.

She hit the pause button and looked up at Arthur. "Did you check the license plate numbers on the vehicles?"

He nodded. "The ones I could collect from the footage. The last SUV is part of the Sacramento office of the governor's fleet, and the highway patrol motorcycles are valid licenses."

Harri started the video again. Her stomach twisted, knowing what was coming. The camera field went dark for instant, then the blurry picture shook violently. The drone zipped sideways and backed away from the bridge.

In time for the last gray SUV to slam into the water surface.

She couldn't watch anymore and looked up at Arthur. "Did you check to see if it was authentic?"

"Mr. Meadowfield received it from an anonymous account twenty minutes after the incident." Despite his firm tone, his body shook. "I'm trying to trace the e-mail routing, but I will need Tim's assistance."

"Where is he?" Susan asked. "With the commotion, he and the twins would normally be charging in here."

"The guys are next door." Harri waved in the direction of the abandoned Canyon Industries headquarters across the street. "Tim's working on teaching Steve how to fight."

Susan cocked her head. "I thought Steve had nixed going into the superhero business."

"Rey's afraid to punch me." Aisha flashed a rueful smile. "So he needs someone of his caliber to practice with."

"That's because domestic violence is a chargeable crime in this state," Harri said.

"Really?" Aisha glared at Harri. "If we're going that route, both Rey and I should be in jail for what went down in Japan last year."

Harri winced at the reminder. Yeah, technically, Rey had been under the control of Professor Paranoia at the time, but getting the supervillain extradited to the U.S. to clear Rey of a domestic violence charge would be a royal pain in the ass.

Not to mention Aisha had given as good as she got in their battle in the Suicide Forest.

Susan planted her palms on the desk and leaned forward. "Harri, play that video again."

As much as she didn't want to see it for the second time, she clicked the play button. And for all of Susan's protests about the illegally obtained footage, she didn't have a problem actually watching it.

Harri looked up at Susan's scrunched features. "What are you looking for?"

"I'm not sure," she murmured.

"You think it could be a deep fake?" Aisha asked.

"I find the coincidence of a drone tracking the governor's motorcade during a supers battle downtown a bit odd in the timing department." Susan didn't take her eyes from Harri's laptop screen.

Harri reached for her receiver and jabbed the speed dial button for Tim's phone. It rang twice before an enormous crash from outside rattled her office windows.

"Cut it out, you two!" Tim yelled in her ear, confirming the tremor was due to the twins. He lowered his voice to a normal level when he said, "What's up, Harri?"

That was her boyfriend, all right. All business during the day as usual. Not at all like he was when he woke her up with soft kisses a few hours ago.

"We've got major issues." She quickly ran down the events of this morning. "I need you and Steve to pack bags. We're heading to San Francisco on the next available flight."

Chapter 4

Aisha watched her husband pace while she fed Mitch his lunch in their loft. As long as he wasn't stomping hard enough to go through the newly refinished floorboards, she wouldn't say anything. It was better he released his disgruntlement by working off his steam in a non-destructive manner.

Like pacing.

"I should be going with Harri, not Steve," Rey muttered for the umpteenth time.

"You decided you wanted to be a cook, not a lawyer," she said gently. "Harri needs a legal assistant in San Francisco, not a personal chef."

He paused in mid-step and whirled to face Aisha. "You're taking Steve's side?"

Mitch squirmed and pulled away, letting her know he was done. She took the towel from her shoulder and cleaned up both herself and Mitch before she transferred both the towel and the baby back to her shoulder.

She eyed Rey as she patted Mitch's back. "I'm not taking anyone's side. We've just introduced Black Falcon and Ghost Owl to Canyon Pointe. Or are you giving up that part of our lives?"

"That's exactly why I should be going." Rey gestured wildly. "What if this is a set-up by Corvus?" Rey had even more of a reason to hate the black ops group than Harri. He was struggling with PTSD for what Professor Paranoia did to him, though he'd never admit it.

"Trubble is sitting in prison as we speak," Aisha said. Mitch punctuated her statement with a giant burp.

"Some of his cronies got away." Rey slammed his right fist into his left palm. "Not to mention, we still don't know who was Trubble's snitch within the NSB. And Steve doesn't know the first thing about fighting if Doctor Liquidation was behind this—"

"Stop it," she snapped. "You need to get over your jealousy. Like now."

Mitch burbled, but it sounded like, "Yeah."

Aisha stood and carefully handed their son and the towel over to Rey. He continued to pat Mitch's back while she put her clothes back in order.

"I get you—" she started at the same time Rey blurted, "I'm sorry—"

They both stopped.

"Go ahead," she said.

"I'm not mad at you." Rey frowned and stared out the windows for a moment. He turned back to her. "You're right. I am jealous. I don't like Harri depending on Steve more than me for her safety."

"Steve accompanying Harri isn't about her protection," Aisha said. "She needs a legal assistant with her, and she's not going to drag Patty along when Grace isn't even a year old yet. Think about who she's taking and who she isn't."

Deep rose flushed across Rey's face as he realized why Harri made the call she did. "None of the parents are going."

"And Susan's staying because I can't handle the entire firm workload by myself." She smiled. "Not even with all my superpowers."

"Do you regret it?" Concern replaced the embarrassment on his features.

"Regret what? Mitch? Hell, no!" she blurted. "I've always wanted a baby—"

"I mean the HRSP," Rey murmured. "And that Xquic made your condition permanent."

Aisha couldn't blame her mother-in-law too much. Xquic had done what she thought was the right thing in order to protect her grandson. Still, it would have been nice if the Mayan goddess had asked first.

"No," Aisha said firmly. "I have you and Mitch out of the deal. I can live with the trade-off." She smiled at him holding their son. "And when a regret even crosses my mind, all I have to do is fly, and it all goes away."

Mitch let out a resounding belch as if he agreed. Both Rey and Aisha cracked up.

"He's definitely your son." Aisha wrapped her arms around her husband's waist. Rey kissed the top of her head.

A knock on the loft door brought reality crashing back in. The restored barn door slid back an inch.

"Safe to come in?" Molly called out.

"Yes," Aisha and Rey said at the same time.

Molly Reinhold, AKA the superhero Nix, pushed the door open and entered. She'd gone back to her natural hair color over the winter, a barrage of purple, blue, and green. However, she kept it short, and wore a platinum blond wig when she was superheroing. Since she didn't have a day job, she made an excellent babysitter for children of super parents.

Especially now that she wasn't going by the moniker Screaming Orgasm.

"Have you guys looked out on the street lately?" Molly said.

"What's going on?" Aisha asked.

"Anti-super protestors," Molly said with a disgusted tone. "The word about San Francisco spread like frickin' wildfire this morning."

"It doesn't help that every news organization in the country keeps replaying that clip of the accident over and over again," Rey muttered. "We should suit up. I'll take Mitch down to Miguel's."

"He's taking Harri and the rest to the airport in fifteen minutes," Aisha said.

"But Javier's here." Rey shifted Mitch to cradle him. The baby beamed at his dad before his eyelids started to droop.

"Two babies is a lot of responsibility for a fourteen-year-old," Aisha protested.

"Trust me," Molly said. "Mitch will be out cold for his afternoon nap for two hours. Javier will be fine until Miguel gets back from the airport."

Aisha sucked in a deep breath to swallow her envy. Molly knew Mitch's schedule better than she did. But for right now, she was the main breadwinner of the family until the residuals from the Black Falcon licensing deals she put together started paying off.

She kissed Mitch on his forehead before she grabbed his portable bassinet and followed her family to the elevator.

Chapter 5

Harri pulled out her laptop as soon as the flight attendants gave clearance for the use of electronic devices. Steve snagged a yellow legal note pad and a pen from his own carryon bag. As much as she wished she could enjoy sitting in first class again, they had too much work to do and barely a two-hour flight.

And frankly she'd much rather be sitting with Tim who was across the aisle and a row ahead of her and Steve.

"Not that I'm bitching or anything," Steve whispered. "But isn't charging first class tickets to a client a little unethical?"

"Normally, I'd agree," Harri murmured. "But these were the only seats available on a direct flight until the red-eye, and I don't want our client indisposed longer than necessary."

Steve nodded. Growing up with his upper-middle class adoptive parents meant he could read between the lines. As much as she loved Rey, he'd be getting on his high horse about unnecessary expenditures right about now.

She opened her e-mail application and read the missive Gil Wilcrest had sent her right before she and her team boarded the jet. For someone who was nearly fifty years older than her, Mr. Wilcrest didn't shy away from modern technology. Steve leaned a little closer so he could read the missive as well.

Dear Ms. Winters:

Per federal regulations, I have not been allowed to speak with your client since I am not the attorney of record. However, I have received a list of charges against your client with the caveat that they are subject to change. They are as follows:

– One count of murder of a public official, to whit Governor Clark DeWine of California
– One count of terrorism, to whit the destruction of the Golden Gate Bridge
– 324 counts of second-degree homicide (this is merely the current body count as recovery efforts are still underway)
– Five counts of negligent destruction of public property (including the Federal Reserve and surrounding buildings)
– One count of obstruction of justice, to whit allowing Doctor Liquidation to escape

NSB has confirmed the object that struck the bridge was in fact one of the vaults from the San Francisco Federal Reserve Building.

Per our telephone call earlier today, I will meet you and your party upon your arrival at the San Francisco airport.

Pleasant journey,

G.A. Wilcrest

"Holy shit," Steve murmured. "I thought superheroes had greater immunity under the liability laws when performing their duties."

"They did until some dumbass attorney came along and started chipping away at that immunity when it came to public damages," Harri muttered.

"Who would do such a thing?" Steve asked.

"Me."

Between the time difference and the longer days of June, the after-noon was bright and sunny in San Francisco when they landed. After they collected their checked luggage, Harri spotted the whiteboard sign sporting "Winters Party" above the crowd near the exit from bag-gage claim. But all she could see was two hands until they pushed past the milling travelers.

An elderly man who was barely her height stood with the sign raised above his head. He looked like the garden gnome that sat on her patio in her old townhouse. A frill of white hair started in the middle of his chin before it climbed up his rosy cheeks, curled over his ears, and disappeared around the back of his head. However, he wore a medium gray suit with a blue and purple striped tie instead of a blue tunic and leggings with a red cap like her statue. He didn't look much different from his website's professional photograph.

She approached him and held out her right palm. "I'm Harri Win-ters, Mr. Wilcrest."

With a genial smile, he lowered the sign and shook her hand. "A pleasure, Ms. Winters, and it's Gil. Mr. Wilcrest was my father."

Harri chuckled at his bad joke. "Then you call me Harri."

He nodded sharply. "Very well, Harri. I took a rideshare here so we could talk in your rental vehicle. I hope you don't mind, but I thought it best not to waste time given your client's reputation and freedom are on the line."

"Not at all." She made introductions with all the men before she frowned. Grandma Harri hated showing any weakness, but dragging an eighty-something attorney and her co-counsel through the San Francisco Airport's concourse didn't seem wise. "Would you like to get started over on one of those benches while we wait for Tim and Steve to get the vehicle?"

"Don't be silly, Harri." He gestured for them to follow him. "The rental kiosks are right this way."

Gil took off at a pace that left Harri slightly out of breath when they reached the car rental company desks. Even Tim had a sheen of perspiration across his forehead, so she didn't quite feel as bad.

The clerk was pleasant until Harri insisted Tim and Steve be added to the rental contract and the gentleman behind the counter checked their driver licenses. He frowned and lowered his voice. "I'm sorry, Ms. Winters, I can't add Mr. Connors as an authorized driver."

"Why not?" Harri growled.

"He's only twenty-two," the clerk whispered.

"I can hear you, you know," Steve said.

"The age limit for rental car drivers is twenty-one," Harri barked.

"I'm sorry, but corporate changed its policy." Surprisingly, the clerk actually looked apologetic, instead of the blank stare of someone just collecting a pay check. "It's now twenty-five."

Harri leaned her elbows on the counter, checked the clerk's nametag, and smiled sweetly. "Darrin, what's your company's policy if a twenty-two-year-old flies one of your vehicles?"

Darrin drew back, appearing thoroughly confused. "Wh-wh-what do you mean?"

"I could have brought one of my clients who's under twenty-five with superstrength and flight capabilities." She cocked her head. "Your company may contractually say my legal assistant can't drive your ve-hicles, but how are you going to stop one of my superhero clients, or a supervillain for that matter, from picking your vehicle and flying some-where with it?"

Darrin licked his lips and nervously glanced at Steve. Luckily, the kid was playing things cool and kept his game face on.

"I-I suppose I can make an exception in this circumstance, but I have to require you to purchase our insurance," the clerk said.

"I was planning on it anyway, Darrin."

The rest of the transaction went smoothly. As they left the rental desk and headed for the exit to the shuttle to their lot, Gil chuckled. "Now I know how you're chipping away at the legislation I drafted to protect superheroes."

"What do you mean?" Harri asked. She stepped through the parting glass doors and breathed in the city's atmosphere. Despite the similar smells of exhaust and fast food as Canyon Pointe's terminal roadways, the air was so much cooler.

"You nibble away at the rules one little bite at a time like a termite." Gil grinned at her.

"Her nickname in law school was the mouse with the mouth," Tim volunteered.

Gil roared while Harri glared at Tim.

"Shut up," she hissed. "Just shut up." She climbed into the shuttle bus, her cheeks burning.

"I wouldn't have gone there, dude," Steve said as he shoved their bags onto the top shelf of the luggage storage rack on the bus. "And don't expect me to protect you from her."

Gil settled next to Harri on the bench. "I'm sorry for laughing, Harri. I had a similar nickname in school."

"You're one of the most respected attorneys in the country," she murmured while she pointedly ignored Tim. "I doubt if yours was that bad."

"I was so nervous during my first moot court I couldn't control my flatulence," Gil said. "I lived with the name of Fartemus for years."

Harri couldn't stop the first burble that escaped.

"It's okay to laugh," Gil said.

She didn't bother trying to suppress the rest of her mirth. Even Steve and Tim were grinning. Once she got herself under control and wiped her eyes, she asked, "How did you escape that one?"

"Time." Gil released a heavy sigh. "Most of my classmates who called me that have passed away."

"I'm sorry," she said.

"Enjoy the time you have, my dear." Gil patted her hand. "It goes by faster than you think."

Harri swallowed hard. She caught Tim looking at her with concern, and she shot him a small smile. All right. She wouldn't kick him out of her room tonight, but she'd definitely find a way to get him back for dredging up her old nickname in front of someone she found herself wanting to impress.

CHAPTER 6

Aisha closed the blinds in her office. She may not be able to see the protestors' signs, but she could damn well hear them with her permanently enhanced senses. When her smart phone rang, she nearly jumped out of her skin. She breathed a little sigh of relief at the caller ID and thumbed the answer button.

"Hey, Qiang."

"Do you need assistance clearing the street?" Qiang Reilly, AKA the superhero Sparx and one of the firm's first clients, never bothered with small talk. It was one of the reasons Aisha liked the acerbic woman.

Harri still hadn't forgiven Qiang after she had been blackmailed into assassinating Harri by Corvus.

"We're fine." Aisha winced as something rebounded off the security glass of one of the front doors to the building. "CPPD are on their way. Did Steve tell you to check on us?"

Qiang chuckled. "Actually, it was Tim. Steve merely said he'd be out of town on business, but with the San Francisco incident all over the news, I didn't have to guess why."

Aisha sat in her office chair as she devoured that bit of news. It was good to hear her brother-in-law was taking this legal internship seriously, and not blabbing firm business to the woman he was pursuing.

"Everyone in the country has seen that clip," Aisha murmured. Another *boing* reverberated through her office.

"Damn, even I heard that without superhearing," Qiang said. "You sure you don't want some help?"

The tenor of the crowd changed to a subdued rumble. Aisha rolled her chair back to the window and peeked between the blinds.

"Black Falcon and Nix just arrived," she said.

"Uh-huh," Qiang drawled. "How long has he been suited up?"

"Since the crowd started forming." Aisha had been a little worried when Miguel's van exited the parking garage. She wasn't sure the protestors would let him pass without causing another incident. Thankfully, they let him by with a few shouts and shaken fists, and he got Harri, Steve, and Tim to the airport on time.

She didn't want to think about what could have happened if school wasn't out for summer. Miguel's son Javier would have walked right into that mess on his way home this afternoon.

No, Javier was smarter than that. He would have ducked into Marta's restaurant or Celia's bodega and called his dad.

"How are your parents doing at Sunny Days?" Aisha said. The sales from the Sparx doll over Christmas had prompted the toy licensor to add additional Sparx products. Then parents started clamoring for their own Sparx gear. The licensing fees from those alone had been enough to pay off Mrs. Tranh's medical and rehabilitation expenses as well as rent an assisted living apartment for Mr. Tranh in the same complex. He could walk the hallways to the Sunny Days rehab section to see his wife any time he wanted, and Qiang didn't have to worry about him driving or collapsing from heat exhaustion during the Canyon Pointe summer.

"You're changing the subject," Qiang accused.

"You don't need to come over to the Lechuza Building," Aisha stated firmly.

"Because?" Qiang prompted.

"Because things are better with your boss since you haven't been missing so many days at work, right?" Aisha reminded her.

"All right." Qiang sighed. "If you insist on discussing personal matters, Cha's actually loving it over there, though he'll never admit it. Mom's rehab therapy is coming along. Her therapist thinks she might be able to move into the apartment by the end of June."

"Are you concerned about the cost?" Aisha asked. Qiang being an accountant made some encounters with her better. Her parents being frugal refugees made other things worse.

"No," Qiang said quietly. "You were right to put the money into a trust for them. They'll be taken care of if something happens to me. I just . . . miss them being at our house."

"Can you take Connor over to see them tonight?" Normally, Aisha didn't get this involved in her client's lives. But with Qiang's day job, her elderly parents, and her autistic son, Aisha wasn't sure how the woman managed to get anything accomplished. And she didn't really have any friends outside of the supers community. Even the other supers were more colleagues and acquaintances to her than friends.

"Conner left for summer camp yesterday, but that's a good idea," Qiang said. "I'll call Cha and take dinner over with me."

Now, that her client and friend sounded a little perkier, Aisha said, "Want some good news or some good news?"

"Isn't that supposed to be good news or bad news?" Qiang laughed.

"Not today," Aisha assured her. "I planned on calling you, but you beat me to the punch."

"Then I'll take the good news first," Qiang said.

"The battery company wants to renew the spokesperson contract, and they want to make it a three-year term." Aisha pulled Qiang's folder from the top of her to-do pile.

"Really?" Qiang lowered her voice. "Do I have to do more commercials?"

Aisha flipped to her notes on the deal. "Yes, but they agreed to your stipulation that any filming takes place on weekends with a maximum of four commercials total."

"Wait a minute." The scratching of a pencil on the other end of the phone call stopped. "I said three."

"They want to premier a special one during a certain Sunday football championship. Your numbers have gone up with males eighteen to sixty-five."

"Oh, wonderful." Sarcasm coated Qiang's voice. "I'm playing to American perverts and their geisha fantasies."

"You're also a major inspiration for all girls, else you wouldn't have sold all those dolls. But back to our original subject." Aisha named the figure the battery company offered.

Qiang squealed. The taciturn woman actually squealed like a little kid. Aisha bit her tongue to keep from laughing out loud.

"Before you get too excited, there's more," she said.

"Okay." Qiang's tone turned tentative, like she was waiting for bad news.

"The Superhero Studios option?"

"Oh, god, it fell through again." Qiang muttered an obscenity, but her tone immediately brightened. "That's okay. I know it's not what we were hoping—"

"Dammit, Qiang," Aisha said. "You're worse than Harri."

"If you're going to insult me—"

"Are you going to let me finish?" Aisha said. After a moment of silence, she continued, "They've picked up the option."

"And?"

"They've signed off on your casting terms that the actress playing Sparx needs to be Asian-American."

"Yes!"

"You're fist-pumping, aren't you?" Aisha chuckled.

"Hell, yes," Qiang said. "What about the script approval?"

"That was Barry and Dino's only stipulation—"

"Oh, my god," Qiang whispered. "Dino Dunberg is directing it?"

"Yep, and they're willing to let you read it, but the script cannot leave my office," Aisha stated. "You'll have to come here to read it. And sign a non-disclosure agreement before you do. They are open to input from you, but only if we're not talking major rewrites because Dino wants to start shooting in August."

"That's less than two months," Qiang murmured.

"Which means you need to get your ass over here one night this week and read it," Aisha said.

"And the points?" Qiang's voice quivered.

"They came down to three like we expected."

"Of-of gross with the executive producer credit?"

"Of gross with Sparx getting an executive producer credit," Aisha confirmed.

"I-I shouldn't be this excited, should I?"

Aisha chuckled. "Girl, you can be as excited as you want to be."

There was no response but panting. Like Qiang was running. Or having really active intercourse.

Concern rolled through Aisha as the weird breathing sounds coming through the receiver got worse. "Qiang, are you hyperventilating?"

"I-I think so."

"Do you have a paper shopping bag?" Aisha's own breathing hitched at the odd sounds Qiang made over the phone. "A lunch bag?"

"Lunch . . . bag." She was gasping.

Damn. Aisha prayed it really was hyperventilation, and Qiang wasn't having a heart attack or something worse. There was rustling on the other end, then the whoosh and crinkle of brown paper.

A terrible suspicion occurred. "Did you just fish your lunch bag out of the trash?" Aisha asked.

"Yes." *Gasp. Crinkle.*

Aisha couldn't help it. She started to laugh. "Qiang Reilly, you are the only person I know who is scared shitless over being set for life."

More crinkling came over the phone line. "You don't understand what my parents went through, Aisha."

"You're right." Aisha said softly. "I don't. But you need to get over your fear of success. As your lawyer, I expect you to keep me in the style to which I've become accustomed."

"You are becoming as bitchy as your partner." But Qiang was laughing again.

"You really shouldn't insult Susan like that. She's a very nice lady." Both women laughed for a moment before Qiang's tone turned more solemn. "I know you can't give details, but is Ultra okay?"

"Harri flew out this afternoon with part of the team."

"Wow." Qiang whistled. "That must have been some argument at the firm this morning."

"There wasn't any argument," Aisha firmly stated.

"Uh-huh." Qiang chuckled. "When you go into ice queen mode, there was a fight. And his name was Rey."

"So now we're going to deliberately flunk our Bechdel test by talking about our men?" Aisha asked.

"It bothers Steve that Rey feels he needs to compete with him," Qiang said. "He wants to have a real relationship with his brother."

"I know, and I believe Rey does, too. He—" Aisha bit her tongue. She'd been trying to get Rey to talk to a therapist specializing in superhero issues. She wasn't a psychiatrist, but she'd lay good money he was suffering from PTSD after everything Professor Paranoia had done to him. But betraying her husband wasn't an option.

Aisha inhaled deeply and released the breath. "He'll get there. It's not like either guy was looking for the other or even had a reason to suspect a sibling existed. This caught them both by surprise—"

Shots rang outside and pinged off the bulletproof glass.

Shit!

"Aisha?" Qiang's alarmed shout meant she was about to take off from her office.

Which would only get her written up by her anal boss.

"Stay put and let me call you back." Aisha thumbed the icon to end the call and concentrated to keep from literally flying out of her chair and into the reception area.

"Where the hell are the police?" she roared as she stomped out of her office.

"They've only just arrived." Arthur stood next to Patty and her chair. They both were watching events on the sidewalk.

Why was it Aisha could scream bloody murder and it didn't faze him, but Harri making a sarcastic comment turned him into a trembling bucket of goo?

"Then what the heck—"

"You might want to go back to your office," Arthur said.

"Why?" Aisha demanded. The intercom buzzed, and she turned toward the front doors.

Both Black Falcon and Nix stood outside, drenched in blood.

Chapter 7

Harri clenched her fists when what she really wanted to do was leap over the desk and pound her client's Miranda rights into the Alcatraz security officer's head. Or throw up on him. The waves had been particularly choppy on the ferry ride to the prison.

It didn't help seeing West Coast supers aid in the victim retrieval by the bridge.

Or maybe it was the prison's force field energy sizzling against her nerves. Even though the federal government had kept the original exterior, the inside had been renovated to match the sterility of every other prison. Except in this case, the interior had been upgraded with materials that were resistant to the powers of Alcatraz's current inhabitants. The reflections from break-resistant layers of the glass and plastic over the titanium hallway made Harri feel like she was in an amusement park funhouse.

"You have no cause to keep my client from their counsel," Harri said as calmly as she could.

Officer Macali's giant moustache twitched. The facial hair could have played its own character in the Star Wars franchise. "Ultramegaperson has been charged with terrorism and assassination—"

"Are you saying their civil rights have been suspended, young man?" The expression on Wilcrest's wizened features appeared more disappointed than angry.

"Of course not—"

"Then let us see them," Harri said.

"W-we can't guarantee your safety, Ms. Winters," Officer Macali finally stammered out.

"Why are you stalling?" she snapped.

"Because I wanted to speak to you first."

Harri whirled to face the man behind her, and she had to quell her shock. Sherman Dowdy, the Attorney General of the United States. There wasn't a damn thing dowdy about the man. He was handsome, charming, and damn good at his job. According to most political analysts, he was more likely to be his party's nominee for president instead of the current vice-president in two years.

"Attorney General Dowdy." Harri inclined her head before she eyed the NSD agents with the AG. "The president felt it was necessary to send in the big guns on this case?"

He didn't flinch at her pointed remark. "No, I did." He gestured to a side hallway. "May we speak privately?"

It wasn't a request, and Harri knew it.

"All right." But when Tim and Steve moved to follow her, the NSD reached for their weapons. Steve immediately stepped between the agents and Harri.

"I wouldn't fire those guns if I were you, gentlemen," she said with a smile.

"Do you plan on breaking Ultramegaperson out of prison, Ms. Winters?" the AG asked.

"My legal assistant and my head of security are concerned about my safety and welfare since the feds lost control of Corvus," Harri replied.

"Besides, weapons aren't allowed inside any federal prison, and neither I nor any of my party have any." She pointed looked at the guns aimed at her.

Or rather Steve.

"Mmmm. I see." Dowdy looked at his security. "Put your weapons away, gentlemen."

The NSD agents reluctantly did so.

The AG grinned at Harri. "I have a feeling neither you nor any of your party need weapons to break Ultramegaperson out of Alcatraz."

"That's true." She grinned back at Dowdy, though she could feel Tim glaring daggers at her. "The only reason my client is still here is because they are a law-biding citizen."

"And because she makes too much money on licensing," the AG said.

"'They,'" Harri corrected. "The proper pronoun for Ultramegaperson is 'they.'"

The charming mask slipped a bit on Dowdy's face. Well, it was good to know where he stood. It also explain why the NSB arrested Ultra this morning. The feds planned to use them for a scapegoat.

It also explained the reason for the private conversation. The feds wanted Harri to drop Ultramegaperson as a client.

Gil Wilcrest cleared his throat. "Unless you have a plea deal you wish us to relay to Ultramegaperson, Mr. Attorney General, we would like to see our client now."

"Mr. Wilcrest, it is an honor to meet you." Dowdy held out his hand.

Gil eyed the outstretched palm, then he looked at the AG's face with that same expression of grandfatherly disappointment. "Son, you would have done better if you'd offered your hand to the lead counsel in our client's defense and addressed her properly."

Harri bit her tongue to keep from chuckling at Gil's reprimand of the AG.

"Fine." Dowdy dropped his hand. "Here's the deal, Harri. Give us the original Ghost Owl, and we'll drop the charges against Ultramegaperson."

This time, she did chuckle. "I can't give you Jatz'om Kuh. He's dead."

"You know how this works with supers, Ms. Winters." Dowdy flashed his incredibly white teeth in a grin reminiscent of a Disney villain. "No body. No death."

"Unless the Mayan goddess Xquic takes both body and soul to Xibalba," Harri said softly.

Dowdy's right eyebrow rose. "Do you really expect me to believe that cock-and-bull story you fed to the FBI?"

"I don't care what you believe." Harri shrugged. "But those FBI agents were present in Westerville Park when everything with the fake Captain Justice went down last year. Not to mention, we live in an age where human beings can fly, so I'm willing to go on a little faith the person claiming to be Xquic wasn't human. And if you have any questions about my encounter with her, I suggest you talk to the FBI agents who were there."

"One of whom was your ex-husband." Dowdy smirked. So much for the charm.

"And another one of whom was one of Corvus's moles." She shrugged again. "Look, Byron Trubble even tried to con me into recruiting the original Ghost Owl for Corvus. But then I'm sure you've already read the transcripts of the former general's trial. Really, Attorney General Dowdy, blackmail doesn't become you."

Behind her, Tim snorted and managed to turn the sound into a coughing fit.

Harri stepped closer to Dowdy and lowered her voice. "And right now, I have to wonder about your relationship with a convicted felon."

While the AG kept his expression neutral, anger sparked in his eyes. "I think you missed your calling, Ms. Winters."

His ploy was so damn obvious. She merely smiled. "I doubt even I could have saved the Winters Department Store chain, but I can damn well save my clients from a frame job."

"That's for the jury to decide," Dowdy said.

"You're right. It is. Assuming the charges against my client actually stick. Now, I suggest you let me speak with Ultramegaperson because—" Harri made a show of checking the time on her phone. "—you won't like my partner's press release that will go out at two p.m. if you don't."

CHAPTER 8

Aisha's stomach clenched at the sight of her husband covered in blood. "Let them in, Patty."

Susan raced out of her office. "I heard gunshots," she said. She turned to the front doors as Black Falcon and Nix entered. At the sight of the two superheroes, she stammered, "Oh, my god."

Aisha's stomach roiled at the coppery odor of not so fresh blood. She swallowed hard to keep the acid and her lunch down as scarlet fluid dripped on the white and black tiles.

"It's not ours," Rey said. "A protestor threw it on us."

"And it's real," Molly wailed. "My wig is ruined!"

"Did you see who did it?" Aisha asked.

"Yeah." Rey grimaced. "The cops arrested her."

"And the shooter?"

"Different guy, also arrested." Rey grimaced. "I was apprehending him when the female protestor got me with the blood."

"And she poured the rest on me when I tackled her," Molly said.

"Is it human blood?" Aisha asked.

"Shit!" Susan stared at her. "What if it's contaminated?"

"Black Falcon, let me grab a couple of tarps to cover you, then fly Nix downstairs," Arthur said. "I'll take samples before you two get into the decontamination shower."

"Together?" Whites surrounded the glitter of Nix's irises. The same mix of colors as her natural hair.

"Yes, of course." Arthur blinked as if he didn't understand the question.

"Just remember my power set if you even think about touching my husband," Aisha growled at Nix as Arthur jogged to his office/workshop. She couldn't tell by their skin colors since they were coated in blood, but both Rey and Molly's expressions looked adequately embarrassed. And Arthur accompanying them would make sure there were no hijinks.

Not that Rey would do anything, but Nix had made her interest in him known before she learned Rey and Aisha were an item. And Nix was much closer to Rey's age than Aisha was.

Arthur rushed out of his office with a couple of canvas tarps, probably leftover from the renovations of the first floor. He carefully wrapped the two superheroes without touching the blood.

"Baby, I—" Rey started.

Aisha held up a palm and said, "Go. We'll talk later."

Thankfully, Rey didn't move at superspeed and fling blood everywhere. He carefully cradled Nix in his arms. Arthur strode to the door to the basement and placed his hand on the biometric lock. The lock hummed and clicked, and he wrenched open the door. Rey floated across the reception area and through the doorway. Arthur pulled the door closed behind them.

Patty pushed to her feet. "I'll go fetch the mop—"

"No!" Aisha and Susan said at the same time.

"We can't take the risk that it's contaminated with something," Aisha said.

"I've got a friend who specializes in crime scene clean-ups," Susan offered.

"Get them over here," Aisha said. "We'll pay whatever surcharge they want." A sick feeling spread through Aisha as Susan headed for her office to make the call. What if that blood had splashed on her or Patty or, heaven help them, one of the children?

"Patty, can you work in Harri's office for now?" Aisha asked. From their assistant's pale face, the same fears running through Aisha's mind were racing through Patty's. She nodded mutely and gathered the materials she needed from her desk.

Aisha strode back to her office, her heels clicking out her frustration. She glanced at the time as she sat back down at her desk and reached for the roll of antacid tablets. One-thirty already, and Harri hadn't called yet. Aisha popped the tablet in her mouth and chewed. The strong peppermint cleared the aftertaste of blood and bile at the back of her throat. A check of the news feeds revealed no one had mentioned the death of the California governor. While Aisha intellectually understood Nella's position as a news producer, this story would bury Ultramegaperson if they didn't figure out how to spin it.

They needed a backup plan in case Harri didn't call until after the deadline. A couple of taps opened a new document. While Aisha typed, she debated the merits of going on the air live herself if Harri didn't call her in the next hour.

⁂

At the sharp knock on her office door, Aisha jumped. She glanced at the clock in the corner of the monitor. She had been so involved in crafting her backup press release that an hour had passed. They were coming down to the wire to get something to Nella.

The door opened, and Rey stuck his head around the corner. His hair was tousled and damp. "You okay?"

"Yeah." However, she frowned at the noises and strange voices coming from the reception area.

"Susan's friend just arrived with his cleaning crew." He gestured to ask if it was okay for him to come in, and she nodded. He entered and crossed to her desk. "If it's any help, Arthur says it was pig blood. He's running some more tests, but with the level of anti-biotics in the blood, it probably came from a butcher."

"I'll give Calvin a call before the end of the day and let him know what we found," she murmured.

Rey merely grunted, which was the most he'd ever say about her ex-husband these days. But then, her current husband was a superhero in the same city where her ex was the district attorney. The two men had to play nice.

At another knock at her door, Aisha yelled, Come in!"

Susan entered with papers in hand. "I've got Tony's invoice, and I need you to co-sign the check."

"Let me see." Aisha held her hand out, and Susan gave her the papers. According to the two-page invoice, Tony had knocked quite a bit off his normal charges. The first feeling of something going right today eased the knot in her stomach.

Or maybe it was the second antacid finally kicking in.

She looked up at Susan. "Why the steep discount?"

"I bribed him with some rare Captain Justice merchandise." Susan grinned.

Rey groaned at the reminder of how spectacularly things had gotten fucked up with his first moniker. But Captain Justice's "death" had made him quite a bit of money.

"Haven't we gotten rid of all that shit yet?" he muttered.

Susan stared up at him in surprise. "Are you joking? That stuff's gold! Have you seen what the CJ action figures are going for on Ebay?"

"Speculators ripping off children," Rey growled.

Aisha finished co-signing the check when her phone set buzzed. She tapped the intercom. "Yes?"

"Harri's on Line 1." Patty's voice didn't have her normal cheerful quality, but then, it'd been a hell of a day for all of them.

"Thanks, Patty." Aisha punched the speaker function and the button next to the flashing light for Line 1. "Hey, Harri. Susan and Rey are in the office with me. Do I have to kick one of them out?"

Instead of laughter, a heavy sigh came through the receiver. "No. Someone's framing Ultramegaperson for the assassination of Governor Clark DeWine."

"We know—" Aisha started.

"U.S. Attorney General Sherman Dowdy just tried to blackmail me," Harri snapped.

Aisha's stomach wound itself back into a knot as Harri relayed her conversation with the head of the federal Department of Justice. Susan stared at the phone set, her face getting redder by the second.

When Harri finished, Aisha murmured, "We knew the FBI and the NSB had been infiltrated by Corvus. Why not the rest of the DOJ?"

Susan dropped into one of the visitor chairs. "I'm more concerned about the sudden change in targets. Trubble was obsessed with Rey and Steve. Why does Dowdy care about the original Ghost Owl?"

"Because he was the one who really took down Corvus," Rey said as he rubbed his beard. "No offense to you ladies, but it was his intel Calvin and Eddie used to put Trubble away."

"Ultramegaperson needs to be our priority at the moment," Aisha said sternly. "How are they holding up?"

"Ultra is doing as well as can be expected." Harri huffed. "Corrections put them in general population, so expect a series of lawsuits from idiots who hurt themselves trying to beat up the new super on the block."

"Great." Susan rolled her eyes.

"Hello, everyone," a gravelly older male voice said. "This is Gil Wilcrest."

"Hey, Gil!" Susan sat up straighter in her chair.

"Susan." He cleared his throat. "In addition to the attorney general's ill-conceived tactic, one of the Navy search and rescue ships discovered the object that struck the Golden Gate Bridge was one of the vaults from the San Francisco Federal Reserve. Doctor Liquidation simply doesn't have the strength to toss such an object."

"Tim . . ." Harri whined.

"I'm pulling the footage from security cameras," Tim said. "It's going to take a little time to go through it."

"Do you need Arthur to do anything on this end?" Aisha asked.

"He already did," Tim answered. "I'll try not to steal too much of his time. How'd the blood tests come out?"

Aisha winced. "You heard about that, huh?"

"Is everyone all right?" Harri said.

"Yes." A machine whirred to life outside of Aisha's office, so she raised her voice. "We've got a cleaning crew sanitizing everything. So, are we going with a standard categorical denial?"

"Yes." Harri sounded tired which only exacerbated her bad moods. "Ultra swears they didn't toss the vault, much anything else remotely that size and weight."

"Tossing things at Doctor Liquidation wouldn't hurt her anyway," Rey said. "She'd just turn into her liquid form if something landed on her. That's probably how she got into the reserve building."

"So right now, the federal prosecutor in San Francisco barely has a circumstantial case." Susan leaned her elbows on Aisha's desk. "Why the hell did they arrest Ultra? You can get them out on bail during the arraignment easily."

"That's the reason for the assassination charge," Mr. Wilcrest said. "That means Ultramegaperson could be held without bail."

"Aisha, can you . . . ?" It was obvious Harri didn't want to mention some of the firm's contacts in front of an attorney she didn't know well.

"I'll check with the twins' mom, and get back to you, but it won't be until tomorrow," Aisha said. If anybody managed to listen in on their phone call, they would assume she was talking about Rey and Steve's biological mother. Most people didn't know Nix and her sister Sourpuss were fraternal twins, or that their mother was the notorious supervillain Miss Purrception.

"Ultra's arraignment is nine tomorrow morning, so we'll be out of pocket during that time—" A giant yawn interrupted Harri.

"Do you need additional help with security?" Tim's worry carried across the signal though he tried to sound confident in front of Rey.

Who rolled his eyes.

While Rey respected the hell out of Tim, their head of security had a tendency to treat Rey like a kid. Which made a little sense because Rey was technically younger than Tim's murdered son would be now.

"We had more than enough volunteers when the demonstrators

showed up," Aisha said. "Once the stunt with the blood is on the news tonight, I don't think I'll be able to keep all our clients away."

"All right, but let us know if anything else happens," Harri said. "No matter how late it is."

"Will do." After their goodbyes, Aisha pressed the button to end the call.

"I know you two." Rey crossed his arms. "What are you really thinking that neither of you want Wilcrest to know?"

"Wait," Susan protested. "You can't possibly think Gil is involved with Corvus."

"That doesn't mean he isn't being used somehow," Aisha said softly. "But to answer your question, baby, it's the obvious blackmail attempt in a section of Alcatraz where everything, and I mean everything, is recorded."

"A feint?" Rey's right eyebrow quirked upward. "Dowdy was testing Harri?"

"Yeah, but the question is why." Aisha shook her head. "And what does he have against us or Ultramegaperson that he believes will counteract Harri filing blackmail charges against him?"

She already knew that question would be gnawing on her brain for the rest of the night.

CHAPTER 9

Harri thumbed the icon on her phone to end the call and stretched. The hotel where Patty made their reservations wasn't five-star, but it was clean and serviceable and very large and blue compared to the cramped, beige spaces she'd endured the rare times she had to travel as the city attorney for Canyon Pointe. Even better, this hotel room had a large desk for her and Steve to use.

Right now though, the famous Gilbert Amadeus Wilcrest sat across from her while Steve was on a food run. Tim, who had been standing beside her during the call, limped to the king-sized bed, removed his shoes, and propped himself against the headboard.

Harri gritted her teeth for a moment to keep herself from saying anything about him being in pain or refusing to bring his cane on the plane. Tim wouldn't appreciate it. Not in front of Gil. Not when someone nearly twice Tim's age was far more mobile than him.

But then, Gil hadn't been taking on supervillains and every day hoodlums for the last twenty-one years by himself.

"Was Ultramegaperson involved with you exposing Corvus?" Gil asked.

"No." Harri rested her chin on her fist. "They hired the firm five months ago."

"So the poor thing is a pawn in the government's grievance against you." Gil shook his head.

"Corvus was an illegal—" Harri began hotly.

"I don't question that." Gil smiled at her. "However, they were a deniable asset to the powers-that-be. One that you were involved in totally disabling."

"Then they shouldn't have stooped to threatening, kidnapping, and murdering my friends' children," Harri spat.

And immediately regretted her words. Bringing up Tim's murdered son Shane in front of him was a major dick move on her part.

She caught his attention and said, "I'm sorry."

"For telling the truth?" A wry smile tilted his mouth. "Don't ever be sorry for that."

"I agree with Mr. Canyon," Gil said. "I wasn't sure what to expect when Susan asked me to assist you. You are, after all, the young lady whose life's mission seemed to be to destroy the protections I pioneered to keep the superheroes from being used in exactly the fashion Corvus employed."

"I don't have a problem with the superheroes being granted certain protections for the work they do." Harri leaned back in her chair and folded her arms over her chest. "I do have a problem with them getting away with using excessive force, just like I would object to regular law enforcement doing so."

"Except you went after their property." Gil tapped his forefinger on the faux wood veneer of the table.

"Remember that excessive force?" She jabbed her finger in roughly the direction of the Golden Gate Bridge. "If Ultramegaperson was responsible, I'd be the first one crawling up their ass for restitution.

Someone shouldn't get away with the wanton destruction of property that doesn't belong to them."

"And what if it turns out Ultramegaperson is responsible?" Gil said. He had that same disappointed grandparent look on his face. The one she'd seen on Grandma Harri's face too many times to count. The one Dad caused with his partying and drug use.

"If they are, we'll deal with it," she said. "For now, I'm taking Ultra at their word."

Banging came from the hotel door followed by Steve's muffled voice. "Need a little help here."

Tim started to rise, but Harri jumped up, waved him back down, and crossed their hotel room. She yanked the door open. Despite all of Steve's powers, bags were sliding from his grip.

She snatched the two about to hit the floor. "Thanks for fetching dinner."

His attention flicked in Tim's direction and back. "No worries. I know my boss. We'll be working late as it is without wasting a couple hours at a restaurant."

"Do you remember being that young and enthusiastic, Harri?" Gil chuckled.

"I don't even remember what I had for breakfast." She carried the bags over to the table and set them down. Steve followed her and did the same.

"An English muffin," Tim said. "But only because I set the plate in the bathroom before she got out of the shower." He accepted the bottle of water Steve handed him.

"It's good you have people looking after you." Gil chuckled. "My wife used to do the same for me."

"She's gone?" Harri passed his pastrami on rye to him.

"Eleven years now." He slowly unwrapped his sandwich. "I miss her every day."

"If you'll excuse me for a moment, I'd like to get out of this monkey suit." Steve entered the adjoining room and closed the door behind him.

Harri pulled out the two salads with grilled chicken, utensils, and napkins from the second bag. She carried one of the salads over to Tim along with a plastic fork and a couple of napkins.

"You think I'm that messy?" He grinned at her as he accepted his dinner.

"Murphy's Law." She gestured at his clothing. "You're in my bed, and you're still wearing your monkey suit."

"All right then." Gil dabbed the corner of his mouth. "Let's assume you're correct, and Ultramegaperson is not the super responsible for launching the vault at the Golden Gate Bridge. Who is strong enough, and still alive, to do so?"

"You think a dead person did this?" Harri paused in removing the lid from her take-out bowl and stared at him.

"No." Gil unscrewed the cap from his green bottle of sparkling water and took a sip. "At least if certain FBI reports are correct. However, if there are two Captain Justices, there is the possibility of more."

"FBI reports regarding supers are classified." Harri stabbed a hunk of chicken with her fork. "How did you read about Captain Justice and his doppelgänger?"

"I called in some favors." Gil shrugged.

"Maybe your so-called favors are the real reason Dowdy showed up at Alcatraz this afternoon." Harri popped the chicken into her mouth.

"That's entirely possible." Gil regarded his pastrami sandwich for a moment. "However, our responsibility is to our client. Now, how are we going to convince the judge to grant bail for Ultramegaperson?"

CHAPTER 10

Aisha's intercom buzzed. Any hope that it concerned another matter was dashed when Patty announced the caller. Summoning extra patience, Aisha picked up the receiver and tapped the button for Line 1.

"Hi, Nella—"

"What kind of bullshit is this, Franklin?"

Aisha winced at the volume of the news producer's voice. "It's not bullshit, Nella."

"A vanilla press release?"

"Nella, get your panties out of a twist, and listen to me for one minute," Aisha said as calmly as she could. When the news producer remained silent, Aisha continued, "I understand you need to run that footage. However, Ultramegaperson did *not* kill Governor DeWine. They're being framed. Harri and her team in San Francisco are doing their own investigation."

After a few more seconds of silence, Nella said, "What do you want from us to get exclusive rights to Ultramegaperson's side of the story?"

Aisha relaxed a bit. Good. Nella was willing to listen.

"Same as usual," Aisha replied. "Keep Ted on a tight leash. Ellie is smart enough to provide a neutral voice until there's something we can give you."

"Look, I know you want to believe your clients, but what if Ul-tramegaperson really screwed up?" Nella murmured.

"Come on, do you really think that?" Aisha let a little irritation slip into her tone. "They've got a twenty-year career. Besides, not even Redwood is that careless."

"Are Nix and Black Falcon okay? I saw the footage from the demonstration outside of your offices."

Aisha smiled at Nella's abrupt change of topic. That meant she'd play along with Aisha. For now, anyway.

"They're both fine. Nothing a shower and a lot of soap couldn't handle." Aisha chuckled. "Though I am going to have to request the protestor pay for their new supersuits unless she wants to be sued. Those things aren't exactly cheap."

"Ouch." Nella paused again before she added, "Keep in touch, and be careful. We don't need Mitch to lose his parents."

"Thanks, Nella."

As Aisha replaced the receiver, a new worry hit her. How did those protesters assemble so fast? And better yet, why?

⎯⎯⎯⎯◈⎯⎯⎯⎯

After Aisha fed Mitch, she loaded him and his infant carrier into his stroller. She didn't feel like cooking after the day she'd had, and a walk would clear her head. With the summer heat, shorts and a light cotton blouse would be far more comfortable. Once she changed clothes, she and Mitch headed for the elevator and rode it to the first floor.

However, Arthur was taking his role as Tim's backup seriously. Maybe a little too seriously. The intercom by the side door to the parking garage buzzed as she approached.

She sighed and pressed the speaker button. "What, Arthur?"

"How did you know it was me?" he demanded. He never got this pissy with Patty or Harri. But then Aisha never threatened him, though she had the ability to cause more damage to their IT manager than either woman.

"Because no one else has been this anal about me leaving the building besides my husband and Tim, and neither of them are in the building right now."

"Oh." Arthur changed his tone. "With the problems today, it's best if you let someone know when you're leaving, where you're going, and when you'll be back. Especially since Rey won't be home until eleven or so."

She hated to admit he had a good point. Harri, Tim, and Steve may have the harder job of clearing Ultramegaperson's name, but the Canyon Pointe office was taking the brunt of the public's ire. "You're right, Arthur. I apologize. I'm heading down to Marta's for dinner. I should be back in an hour or so."

"All right then. Have a good evening." The intercom clicked.

Some instinct told Aisha he'd be glued to his computer, watching the outside security cameras until she and Mitch came home.

She pressed her hand against the biometric lock. At least, it was finally working right. The HRSP hadn't changed her fingerprints, but it not only changed her natural bioelectric frequency, but the reading wasn't steady until she finally delivered the baby. Tim had a hell of time keeping his damn sensors adjusted for her.

The lock clicked, and Aisha wrestled the stroller past the heavy door. It wasn't a question of strength but awkwardness in getting the baby outside without damaging him or the building. She pushed the stroller down the ramp to the sidewalk. A few of the demonstrators' signs had been hung on the chain-link fencing across the street that guarded what had been the Canyon Industries headquarters over twenty years ago.

She wasn't sure what bothered her more, the nasty hand-drawn missives or the fact that the property was still hung up in court. Rey wanted to purchase the block and construct low-income housing for his fellow squatters now that he had the money to help change people's lives. But even though the owners, like disgraced former Canyon Pointe mayor Quentin Samuels, were in prison, their company, which actually held the title to the property, had been dumped into a receivership by Judge Clemmons. Now, the receivers had filed for a Chapter 11 bankruptcy in order to reorganize the business, a move to try to save the jerks' property from the multitude of personal injury and fraud lawsuits as well as contract disputes after the shady financial dealings came to light.

Vehicle traffic in this part of Canyon Pointe was negligible this time of the evening while Aisha pushed the stroller down to Marta's restaurant. The homeless bobbed their heads and said, "Evening, Miz Aisha." The boys who would be gang members in other parts of the city nodded while their mothers and girlfriends peeked and cooed at Mitch. This was Rey and Miguel's territory, and no one messed with the superhero turned short order chef or the contractor who kept their parents employed.

And even if someone thought about messing with Rey or Miguel, there was still Jatz'om Kuh, the Ghost Owl, to contend with.

The tiny parking lot next to Marta's was half-full when Aisha approached the taqueria's entrance. Even though the sun was still up, the surrounding buildings blocked the last of its rays. Strings of multi-colored lights sparkled around the windows and door in the fading sunshine. More lights were wrapped around the four short palms that graced the corners of the parking lot.

An older couple exited the restaurant, and the gentleman held the door open for Aisha. They both murmured their greeting in Spanish, and she responded in kind. Inside the taqueria, blessed cool air filled the tiny dining room.

"A booth for two?" Marta grinned and grabbed a place mat and a set of napkin-wrapped silverware. She didn't bother with a menu. Not for anyone from the Lechuza Building. She had the residents' favorite dishes memorized, but occasionally, she got them to try something new.

"Yes, please."

Marta led her back to what everyone jokingly referred to as "Tim's spot". It was the one booth where the occupants could keep an eye on all the doors and windows as well as the other diners. Aisha found herself taking Tim's paranoia a little more seriously after everything that had happened over the last year.

Aisha detached Mitch's infant carrier and slid it into the back of the booth. He was already out cold with his post dinner nap. Meanwhile, Marta laid the silverware and place mat on the table before she seized the stroller and folded it like a pro. She tucked it on the opposite bench. Aisha had given up trying to stop the taqueria owner from doting over her. At least, Marta had finally stopped giving Aisha free meals after she broke up a robbery at the restaurant last year.

Aisha pulled her phone out of her left shorts pocket and checked her messages. Nothing new from Harri. The large screen television over the register ran the Action 12! News twenty-four-hour channel with the sound off and the captions on. She didn't need to hear Ted Meadowfield or Brian Mason's voices. Not tonight. Not when they were still pulling bodies out of San Francisco Bay.

Instead, she tried to focus on her to-do list for tomorrow.

"Your dinner, Mrs. Garcia."

She looked up at Rey, and he kissed her. Damn, she could get totally lost in those golden eyes of his. But she looked down at her plate. "That's not my chicken taquitos and guacamole."

"It's something new." He pushed the stroller over and slid into the opposite bench. "Let me know what you think, and be honest."

Two burritos lay on her plate. They were covered in a dark sauce and what looked like pickled red onions and cooked plums. She cut into the right burrito. It was filled with steak, white rice, and diced celery.

Sucking up her courage, Aisha forked a bite into her mouth and chewed. It was more Americanized Chinese than Americanized Mexican. But the steak was perfectly seasoned and grilled.

She swallowed and eyed Rey. "Is that Szechuan sauce?"

He nodded.

Aisha never pictured herself as a foodie, but living with someone who loved to cook meant trying some interesting combinations. "This is one of your better experiments." She dug into her supper.

"It is one of Reuben's creations. I was worried about replicating it." But Rey was grinning, obviously pleased that she liked the unique take on fusion cuisine.

"I take it you heard from him?" She raised an eyebrow as she took another bite.

Rey nodded, turning serious. "He texted the recipe earlier today. He got an 'A' for it in class and wanted to see how it played in the neighborhood. Marta agreed to let me make it tonight's special."

"Is he excited about coming home?" She reached for her water. The heat of the sauce was beginning to hit her.

"Yeah." Rey grinned again and shook his head. "He loves Europe, but he's getting a little homesick."

"This is great." She pointed at her plate with her fork. One burrito was already gone, and she barely remembered eating it all. "But you can't just change Marta's into a fusion place. The regulars aren't going to be happy about it."

"The fusion place is down the road." He looked over his shoulder to make sure no one was listening before he turned back to face her. "We're holding off until we can get control of the land across the street." He made a face. "If we can."

Aisha laid her left hand over his right. "It'll happen when it happens. We've got some leverage in the bankruptcy case. And if we can force the estate into Chapter 7, it will have to liquidate."

"A lot of my friends are still living in that damn hotel," he murmured.

"Hey, you tried to get them out—"

"But their damn, stupid pride shouldn't matter when it comes to their children—"

"Stop," Aisha ordered. "You didn't make them obey you when you were living there. Why do you think you should make them obey you now?"

"I just—" He jerked from her hold and clenched his fists.

"I know you want to make everything right, baby." She laid down her fork. "You want to share your good fortune with the people you care about. But unless you want to become a total asshole like Seismic Shift, you can't *make* people do what you want."

His cheeks puffed as he blew out a deep breath. "Intellectually, I understand that."

"You wouldn't be a true American male if you didn't totally deny your emotional side," she teased.

He laughed at the absurdity of her statement, as she intended. "Fine. I'll get off my white horse. There is something I can make you want." He winked as he rose, and he headed back to the kitchen.

She finished the second burrito. It really was excellent. She just hoped all of Rey's plans could come to fruition. He wanted to revitalize the Canyon Block, which included the eight blocks that surrounded the old Canyon Industries headquarters and the Canyon Hotel. He wanted to give back to the community that lost everything in the collapse of Canyon Pointe's largest employer twenty years ago. Rey was the idealist she thought Calvin had been when they met in law school.

The kitchen door swung open, and Rey presented her a larger than normal bowl. Reuben had taken Arthur's chocolate mousse recipe and created a marvel of fluffy chocolate, coffee, cinnamon, and semi-sweet chunks in a crushed dark chocolate shell.

She grinned. "You know the way to my heart."

"I need to get back to work before Anna burns any more whitefish," he murmured before he pecked Aisha on the lips. She couldn't help watching his ass as he stalked back into the kitchen. She dipped her spoon into the creamy goodness. Maybe she should have gotten the mousse to go. There were some interesting things she could do with it when Rey got home from work.

CHAPTER 11

Harri checked the time on her phone. No wonder she was exhausted. She would normally have been curled next to Tim on the couch and reading an hour ago while he watched the Copperheads game on TV.

Tim had fallen asleep shortly after dinner. That prompted Gil to leave an hour later, once they had a plan of action for the morning's arraignment. Harri and Steve moved into his hotel room to work. Despite the closed door between the adjoining rooms, Tim's snores echoed through Steve's room.

The kid glanced at the door and back at Harri. "Does he always snore this loudly?"

She grimaced. "Only when he overdoes things."

"He might want to look into a sleep study." Steve leaned back in his chair and stretched his arms over his head. "It did wonders for my dad. His CPAP helps him get a better night's rest, and Mom stopped sleeping in the spare bedroom."

"Well, let's call it a night." Harri powered down her laptop. "We're are ready as we're going to be for this arraignment."

Except Steve wasn't paying any attention to her. He had swiveled his chair around and now stared out the window at the bright spot in the distance. The one where the Green Gill was still retrieving bodies from the bay. He was the only U.S. super who could breathe underwater. According to the news, the count was currently at 406.

"Penny for your thoughts," she said.

"Did I make the right decision, Harri?" Steve said softly.

"What do you mean?"

He gestured toward the opposite side of the bay. "I could have been out there today—"

"Yes, you could have, but you can have all the powers in the world, and you still can't stop people from doing stupid shit. Or from dying."

"Advice you've given Rey?" Steve swiveled his chair to look at her. A wistful smile crossed his face.

"No," she said. "I'm paraphrasing Grandma Harri. It's something she told me, often while my dad and stepmom were in jail or rehab drying out after a bender."

Steve swiveled in his chair back towards the window to gaze at the bay again. "Sometimes life's all just a matter of luck, isn't it?"

"Sometimes, it is."

He twisted back to face her. "I guess that's why Aisha's Aunt Queenie told me to seize life by the throat."

"Oh, god!" Harri placed her hand over her heart. "Queenie's dishing romance advice out to you, too?"

"So, she does it to everyone, hmm?" Steve grinned. In some ways, he looked and acted like Rey, but when he smiled, it definitely wasn't Rey's sweet, shy expression.

"She always has seized life," Harri said. "And dished out advice whether you wanted it or not. She's also the person who yanked me aside when Eddie and I were engaged and told me not to marry him."

"Wow!" Steve's eyes widened. "That's harsh."

"Except she was right." Harri chuckled. "We are way too much alike and too stubborn to compromise."

Steve chuckled along with her for a moment before he cleared his throat. "Would it be all right if my parents came to Canyon Pointe this summer?"

"Of course they can come!" She hesitated as she realized why he was discomfited. "I'll let Tim and Arthur know so they can set up security to let your folks come and go. Would a group function make it easier to do the introductions without Qiang wigging out and accusing you of pressuring her?"

Deep rose flushed Steve's cheeks. "I was thinking the Fourth of July party at Marta's restaurant would be a good excuse, and we could watch the stadium fireworks from the roof of our building."

"You are one slick romantic." Harri shook her head. "Plus your parents are a good excuse to stay at her house while Connor bunks with the Esperanza boys."

"You don't think it will work?" Panic replaced his embarrassment.

"I'm the last person to ask for advice on how to get into Qiang Reilly's pants." Harri stood up, and her muscles and joints reminded her how much sitting she had done the entire day. "Don't push too hard, and you'll be fine. However, you can always give Aunt Queenie a call if you're that worried."

Harri grinned at the kid and took two steps toward the door to hers and Tim's room when something crashed on the other side of the closed door. She lunged for the lever, but Steve grabbed her and pulled her back.

He put a finger over her lips before he pointed at the door and then tapped his ear.

Crap. Someone had just busted into hers and Tim's room.

CHAPTER 12

Rey held the taqueria door open for Aisha while she rolled Mitch's stroller out into the sidewalk. Heat still radiated from the surrounding concrete though darkness had fallen over the city. Marta had insisted Rey walk his family home for their safety. The proprietress had assumed Aisha's powers had disappeared after Mitch's delivery, and Aisha had done nothing to disabuse her or anyone else in the neighborhood of that notion. It was better if no one even conceived Aisha was the new Ghost Owl.

"We'll be able to do this more often once Reuben returns from France," Rey murmured.

Aisha looked up at him. "What about him training you? That's going to eat into your free time."

"What if we went to Paris for a few months?"

She paused in mid-step at the sudden change of subject. "I didn't know you wanted to go to the Sorbonne yourself." Guilt flooded through her. "Did I miss something you said? Things have been so crazy with the baby and the new clients—"

"No, this is the first time I've mentioned it to you." He leaned over and kissed her forehead. "And I didn't mean let's go right this minute."

"Oh." Aisha almost felt . . . disappointed by his answer. She'd fantasized about taking a sabbatical in Europe, but her ex-husband always said it wasn't the right time. Funny how he made time for exotic vacations with the new wife and children.

Rey wrapped his arm around her waist, banishing her resentful thoughts, and tugged her into motion again. "We both know Harri can't handle certain clients without you. Emilio asked about joining our restaurant plans. If he's serious, I'd send him to school first. And if he, Dom, and 'Cisco are all away at school, Miguel will need some additional help until next spring now that construction is picking up in the city. And I want to wait until Mitch is old enough he would get something out of such an experience abroad."

"How old?" Aisha crossed her fingers. *Please don't say when he's a teenager.*

"I was thinking maybe somewhere between his first and second birthdays so he could pick up French without too much trouble." Rey grinned down at her. "You could work remotely for a little while. Besides, Miguel's already finished the second floor offices at the Lechuza Building, and you, Harri, and Susan have been considering hiring an associate this year."

"So, definitely after Martin and Renata's wedding?"

"Oh, hell, yeah!" Rey nodded vigorously. "We're not missing your brother's wedding. So, what do you think about us moving to France for a few months next year or the year after?"

Aisha was grinning like a fool, and she knew it. Harri, being her ever-loving control-freak self would throw a bit of a hissy fit, but if Aisha pitched it as possibly expanding the firm, maybe it would take the edge off. And Rey was right. Most of the clients' contracts could be dealt with remotely. Susan could handle anything that required facetime.

It sounded like a dream come true, but there was always a catch. Aisha looked up at him. "There's got to be a hitch to this plan."

"I don't think so, but there's something else I need to discuss with my attorneys." He sucked in a deep breath and released it. "There are some folks who'd like to invest in the businesses we hope to launch—"

A dusty white delivery van screeched to a halt beside them, the side door of the vehicle already opening. Two masked figures in black jumped out, but the clothing they and the driver wore didn't look like any tactical gear Aisha recognized. Nor did she recognize the odd weapons they carried either.

"Don't move, big guy," the first figure ordered. Their voice was distorted by some kind of voice modulator. "Or the missus and the baby die."

"Lady, get the baby, and get in the van." The second figure waved their gun.

Rey tried to edge between Aisha and the stroller and the two goons, keeping his hands up all the while. "Look, if you want money, take my wallet—"

"Shut up!" The first figure pointed at the brick building by the left side of Rey's head and touched a button on their weapon. Some kind of green plasma flashed from the tip of the device.

Aisha automatically bent over to protect Mitch. If her son was anything like her husband and brother-in-law, he wouldn't develop his powers until he was a few years older. There was a loud *zap*. Shards of bricks and mortar bounced off her skin and skittered across the concrete sidewalk. She coughed at the dust, thankful she'd raised the infant carrier's screen against the night insects out of motherly precaution.

"Talk again, and I won't deliberately miss." The first goon pointed their weapon squarely at Rey's chest.

"Lady, we won't ask again." The second goon gestured for Aisha to get Mitch and get in the van.

She considered her options. These assholes didn't seem to know anything about them, but she didn't want to take a chance their plasma weapons could actually hurt her or Rey. Moving at superspeed with Mitch was too dangerous. He wouldn't be able to handle the G-forces. And those plasma weapons would definitely kill her baby if she or Rey made the wrong move. She prayed Rey would play along with the goons for now.

"If you're going to kill me and my son, I want to know why," Aisha snapped, but she unlatched the infant carrier from the stroller.

"Don't want to kill you," the second goon said. "We just need someone's attention. Someone who has a thing for kids."

"Yeah," the first goon affirmed. "Big guy, tell the real Ghost Owl we want to talk to him."

"The original Ghost Owl is dead," Aisha murmured as she reached for her purse in the basket on the back of the stroller.

"Stop arguing. Leave the bag here and take your phone out of your shorts' pocket and leave it, too," the second goon ordered.

"At least, let me take his diaper bag," Aisha said through gritted teeth as she pulled out her phone and laid it on top of her purse.

"No. We have supplies for you and your baby," the second goon said.

Damn. These guys didn't have the professional air of Corvus's minions, but they were being thorough. And the second goon seemed to have a little compassion. Maybe she could use that to her advantage.

Aisha looked up at Rey. He obviously wanted to pound these guys into the concrete for threatening her and Mitch. She gave a slight shake of her head and raised her eyes skyward. He closed his eyes and gave her a nearly imperceptible nod.

The bad guys understood the original Ghost Owl's buttons, which meant she'd never get them to agree to leaving Mitch behind. This would be so much easier if she were their only hostage.

"Stay alive," Rey murmured. She felt him shove something hard and rectangular into the back of her shorts. He tugged her shirt down to hide what was probably his phone in her waistband. She forgot just how many tricks he'd picked up while living on the streets.

Against her better judgment, she climbed into the windowless van with her baby. There was only a dirty piece of carpet to sit on in the cargo compartment. It would be marginally better than the equally gross steel floor. She grimaced before she settled with the infant carrier on the filthy material. If nothing else, she was going to take her dry cleaning bill out of the bad guys' hides.

The second goon jumped in and sat between her and the van's rear door.

"Tell Ghost Owl we'll call his attorneys with the time and place for the meeting," the first goon said before they hopped into the van and slammed the sliding door shut. The driver gunned the engine, and the van peeled down the street with squealing tires and the stench of burning rubber.

Now, why the hell was someone looking for Jatz'om Kuh, the original Ghost Owl? Even worse, why did someone suspect he was still alive?

Whatever was going on, if they believed a woman scorned was bad, the bad guys were about to find out how pissed off a new mom could be.

CHAPTER 13

Harri's heart thudded in her chest, and blood rushed in her ears. Her body would certainly give her and Steve away if anyone with Tim had superhearing. And what if the people who'd broken into her adjoining hotel room were killing Tim while she simply stood here?

Steve dragged her over to her bag, fished out the Taser Tim had designed for her, and pressed it in her hand. Normally, she'd protest the manhandling. But now, she could also hear the low male voices in the other room, though she couldn't make out the exact words.

Once again, Steve tugged her arm. He pulled her to his bathroom. With hand gestures, he indicated for her to stay inside.

Harri did as he asked while he slipped out of the main door of his room. She hated the fact that she couldn't stop her hands from trembling. It made sense for Steve to try to catch whoever was in her room unawares. He had the invulnerable skin, not her or Tim, which brought her fear full circle.

She wasn't a religious person, but she found herself praying Tim was still alive. He'd given up his vigilante ways in favor of training the superheroes who were her clients. He helped take down the people involved in his wife and son's murders, and he's stopped being the Ghost Owl like he promised. He'd done it so the two of them could have a future.

A door opened. Not the door to the hallway. The one to her adjoining hotel room. Steve?

No, he would have called out that it was okay to come out of the bathroom.

Shit. They should have locked the door to her room. But if they had, the bad guys would have known she and Steve were aware of their presence.

An odd clicking started in the bathroom. It was her own teeth. She clamped her jaws and held her breath. She could stay in here and wait for the bad guy to find her, or . . .

Harri stepped out of the bathroom. A hooded figure in black paused at the foot of the closest standard bed.

The hooded man raised his gun. Harri dove for his legs and fired her Taser at him at the same time. The sound of the bad guy's pistol going off was deafening in the small hotel room, but she still heard his shriek of pain through the ringing in her ears as he collapsed on top of her.

CHAPTER 14

Aisha winced as another jounce resulted in the van floor ramming her vertebra together. Her skin may be practically impenetrable and her bones stronger than normal, but that didn't totally prevent internal injuries.

As she'd found out the hard way in Japan last year.

If she counted the turns correctly, they were headed out into the desert northwest of Canyon Pointe. Another hard jounce rattled her teeth. The crappy roads confirmed the van was definitely in one of the surrounding counties.

Mitch whimpered at the rough ride. Aisha lifted him out of the infant carrier and cradled his tiny body.

"How much longer?" she asked.

The goon in the back said nothing.

"Look, you said you had baby supplies."

"We will," they growled.

Time for a different tactic. "What makes you think Jatz'om Kuh is still alive?"

The goon chuckled. "You know the rules of the supers game. No body, no death."

"He was taken by the Mayan goddess Xquic when she took the fake Captain Justice," Aisha said. "There was no body to bury."

"And how do you know this?" The goon didn't sound like they doubted her. Their statement was more matter of fact.

"My law partner was with the FBI team who witnessed the events out at Westerville State Park," she said.

"Sure, she did." Now, they were mocking her.

"If you hadn't made me leave my phone behind, you could have asked her yourself," she said mildly.

"Shut up, you two!" The asshole Aisha thought of as Goon Number One glared at them over their shoulder. Or that's what it felt like though Aisha couldn't see their eyes. "The boss said we're not talking to anyone but the original Ghost Owl."

"And I'm telling you, my partner at the office can't produce the original Ghost Owl," Aisha snapped. "All your threats mean nothing. This kidnapping was for nothing!"

"But the boss is betting the new Ghost Owl will show up," the driver spoke up for the first time. "And when he does, he'll tell us where the old man is."

A little sliver of relief slipped past Aisha's worry. The goons didn't know she was the new Ghost Owl. She'd taken a chance with her licensing image and intentionally didn't make it gender specific. In fact, parents could order the base twelve-inch action figure in any skin tone, gender, hair style, etc. to match their child's visual appearance. But once the action figure was dressed in its superhero costume, there was no way to judge the action figure's gender or race. Anyone could be the Ghost Owl. The initial retail numbers proved the idea was popular, but the real test would come with the holiday sales in a few months.

But she wouldn't know if she couldn't get out of this mess.

"What part of 'shut up' do you people not understand?" Goon

Number One waved their plasma weapon carelessly in the direction of the goon behind the wheel.

"Please don't shoot our driver," Aisha begged. "I don't want to die in a stupid car accident."

Goon Number One swung the end of their weapon toward her. "So you want your face melted off?"

"I don't want any of us to die," Aisha said firmly. "If something happens to me or my baby, do you realize it won't just be the Ghost Owl after you, but all of my clients?"

"So he is alive." Goon Number One's tone had a triumphant note despite the voice changer in their mask.

"The new Ghost Owl does things by the book, and they are a client."

"So is he the son of the original?" Goon Number Two leaned forward. "Is he out for revenge for his father's death?"

"What? No!" Aisha's denial was louder than she intended. Mitch's face crumpled, and he started wailing.

"Now, see what you two did," the driver grumbled. "I'm sorry, Ms. Franklin."

"So you do know who I am," Aisha grumbled as she tried to sooth Mitch.

"In all fairness, the boss said to grab the first kid to leave the Lechuza Building tonight." Goon Number 2 actually seemed apologetic.

On one hand, Aisha wanted to smack all three idiots. On the other, she was glad they didn't try to grab any of the other children living in the apartments in her building. Miguel admitted poor little Francisco still had nightmares from when Seismic Shift kidnapped the boy last year to use as bait to murder Harri.

"It'll be all right," Aisha crooned in Spanish. If they got out of this situation, she was definitely going to say yes to Rey's idea of living in Paris. She didn't care what tantrum Harri threw. She'd never done anything for herself, and damn it, she wanted both Rey and Mitch to see the world.

Hell, she'd be ecstatic to see Japan without Xibalban demons or her mind-controlled husband trying to kill her.

"So what do you think about Daddy's idea to move to Paris?" she murmured in her son's ear.

"You're moving to Paris?" Goon Number Two said. In the front passenger seat, Goon Number One groaned loudly, but they didn't point their weapon at Aisha again. Goon Number Two ignored their associate and continued excitedly, "Have you been there before? I've always wanted to go."

Aisha sagged. She unconsciously switched to back to English as she rubbed Mitch's back. But, hell, if she was making some inroads with one of her abductors, she needed to capitalize on it.

"No, I've never been to Europe." A whisper of grief floated through her. "My best friend's grandmother wanted to take us, but her cancer advanced faster than her doctors anticipated. She died the week we were supposed to leave."

"That's terrible," Goon Number Two murmured. "I want to go to France after all this is over. I always wanted to see the Louvre."

The van slowed and made a left turn. Tires crunched over gravel, and the engine whined as they climbed. Aisha hoped the motor held out. Mitch wasn't wearing anything warm enough to handle the night and altitude's drop in temperature. At least, his crying had died to an occasional whimper and hiccup.

A few minutes later, the van's brakes squealed as the driver brought the vehicle to a stop. Goon Number One hopped out of the passenger seat. The side door slid back, and they waved their weapon.

"Come on. Get out, Ms. Franklin."

Aisha settled Mitch back in his infant carrier and carefully crawled out of the van, the carrier firmly in her clutch.

The stars twinkled brightly against the black velvet sky except toward the east. The faint glow of Canyon Pointe threw up enough light pollution to look like a fake moonrise. But even with her enhanced sight, she didn't spot a super in the air, following the van.

Dammit, Rey! Where are you?

His phone was still tucked in the back of her shorts' waistband. Her abductors might just pat her down. Or the phone could ring with an alert. Or worse, her abductors were jamming the cell signal, and Arthur had no way of tracking her.

The van was parked next to a two-story mountain cabin, the faux log kind that rich people built as their summer retreat from the city and its heat. The kind that made people with money think they were roughing it though they had running water, indoor toilets and electricity.

Exterior lights blinked on, and someone stepped out onto the porch. Like the three who'd kidnapped Aisha and Mitch, she wore black, oddly-designed clothing, but she didn't bother with a hood or a voice modulator. She was white, and her brunette hair was pulled into a tight bun.

"Park the van inside the garage," she ordered. "And bring our guests inside."

Well, they weren't stupid. Hiding the van in the garage would make it harder for anyone to spot the vehicle from the air. Had Rey memorized the plate number as the bad guys sped off with her and Mitch? Or had there been enough dirt to obscure the plate?

Too many questions swirled at super speed through her brain. All she could do was play along until she conceived an escape plan that wouldn't get her baby killed.

Aisha followed Goon Number One up the three steps to the cabin's huge front porch. A swing hung on the left side. A five-piece set of patio furniture sat the right. The front door didn't have any extra security other than a deadbolt and a standard alarm system.

The unmasked woman led the way to the back of the house. Aisha couldn't really call it a cabin anymore since it was easily 4,000 square feet. Only one of the masked idiots followed them.

When they entered the family room, Aisha gasped. The white woman curled up on the couch had exquisite neon blue hair pulled into a tight bun just like her minion. However, she wore white yoga pants and a blue tie-dyed t-shirt, and her feet were bare. She set aside her tablet and rose.

"I apologize for this unconventional meeting, Ms. Franklin." The woman held out her hand. "I'm Doctor Liquidation, and I desperately need to find the Ghost Owl."

CHAPTER 15

Harri could feel the heat rising in her face. Her assailant glared at her while they waited for law enforcement to arrive. Thank god, he was securely tied to one of the hotel chairs in Steve's room. Otherwise, she would have been dead meat. The hotel security seemed confused about what to do, but they were totally happy to wait for the real cops. Meanwhile, Tim and Steve could not stop laughing over the fact she'd tasered her assailant in the balls.

The crash in her room had been Tim smashing a lamp over his other assailant's head. She wanted to throw the fact the two men had gotten the jump on him in his face, but doing so wasn't fair since he'd been sound asleep.

And he was now holding ice wrapped in a hand towel to his cheek while he sat on the bed closest to the door to their adjoining room. He was going to have one hell of a black eye tomorrow morning.

Her assailant's partner was tied up in hers and Tim's room, but between the lamp and Steve's punch, he was out cold. They unmasked both men, but nobody recognized either one. Steve took pictures of them to send back to Arthur so he could scan the law enforcement databases and hopefully identify these two idiots.

Harri folded her arms over her chest and glared back at her assailant. "Why'd you break into my room?"

The bad guy remained silent.

"Dude, she will taser you in the balls again," Steve said as he messaged the pictures to Arthur.

"He's not joking," Tim added. "You should have seen what she did to a wetworks specialist on our first date."

"Was this the electrocution I heard about?" Steve said.

Harri rolled her eyes. Of course, he'd bring up the time she smashed a vase filled with water and roses over his girlfriend Qiang's head and short-circuited the woman's powers.

"No, this was the three-man team. She maced the first guy, I handled the second, and she took out the third guy with a peanut butter pie." Tim grinned.

Steve groaned. "Don't tell me you took her to Nolan's, and she wasted a perfectly good peanut butter pie."

It bothered Harri she *had* wasted the fancy restaurant's famous dessert. Grandma Harri took her to Nolan's often when she'd been little just for a slice of their delicious pie.

"Oh, it gets better. The jerk was allergic to peanuts." Tim laughed at the memory.

"Technically, I did shock him with his own cattle prod while he was looking for his epinephrine," she said.

Even the two hotel security people snickered at that statement. However, the bad guy seemed totally unimpressed with her badassery when it came to sweets.

Harri nudged their prisoner's foot. "What about you? Any allergies I should be aware of before the cops get here?"

"We'll be out on bail in a couple of hours." Her assailant sneered.

Harri leaned closer to him. "And this little screw-up means we're forewarned your boss wants us out of the way. I doubt your boss will be too happy about that. In fact, you might just be safer with us."

A sharp bark of laughter erupted from the man. "You think you're hot shit because you took down B.S. Trubble, don't you?"

"His people came a lot closer to killing me than you did." Harri grinned at him. "And I don't have superpowers."

"Your luck's gonna run out eventually," he said, voicing her own fear.

Banging came from the main door of Steve's hotel room. He went to answer it, and two beat cops sauntered inside.

"Why does this look like it's above our paygrade?" The white male cop pushed back his cap and scratched his forehead.

"They tased me!" The bad guy tried to look like the aggrieved party.

"Because you tried to shoot me," Harri snapped.

"I would've tased you, too," the black female cop said. She looked younger than her partner, but by her stance, she was the senior of the two officers.

"Thank you," Harri said.

"Sisters gotta stick together." The female cop made a face. "Where'd you get him?"

"You'll have to pull down his pants to see the prong marks," Tim offered.

The female cop turned to Harri. Her name tag said Bishop. "Thought you said he tried to shoot you."

"He did," Harri protested.

"But if you tased him in the ass—" Officer Bishop started.

"That's not where the prongs hit him." Blood roared in Harri's face, and her cheeks grew hot again. Officer Bishop and her partner looked at Harri expectantly. Tim and Steve remained silent, as did the two ho-tel security people, but all of the men wore smirks except her assailant.

"The bitch tasered me in the nuts," their prisoner roared.

Bishop's partner stepped closer to the wall between the bedroom and the bathroom. "Hey, Bishop. Check this out."

She peered closer at the drywall. "That sure looks like a bullet hole to me."

"That was there before I got here," the prisoner said.

Both cops looked at him with disgusted expressions.

"Where's the gun?" Officer Bishop asked.

"On the desk." Steve waved at the clear plastic zippered baggie by Harri's laptop. She'd need another baggie for the flight home. There was nothing worse than toiletry bottles spewing their contents all over a woman's underwear in the lower interior air pressure of a jet in flight.

"Did any of you touch the gun?" Bishop asked as she crossed to the desk.

"No," Tim said. "I picked it up with a pen through the trigger guard and dropped it in the baggie."

Bishop opened the zipper with a snap and sniffed the contents. "It's definitely been fired recently." She reached for her radio and called in the incident.

"What do we do while we wait for the techs?" Bishop's partner asked.

"Handcuff him and read him his rights." Officer Bishop laid the baggie on the desk and crossed over to their prisoner. "Unless of course, you want to try to escape. In which case, I'll let the cute white lady tase you again."

The bad guy decided to exercise his right to remain silent.

On the plus side, the hotel manager was so horrified by the incident, he upgraded Harri's party to a two-bedroom suite on the top floor and accessible only by keycard. The minus side was going through the grilling by San Francisco detectives, or inspectors as they rather liked to be called.

Needless to say, they weren't as sympathetic as Officer Bishop.

In the end, the two jerks who broke into Harri and Tim's room refused to talk without an attorney. The inspectors had no choice but agree that Harri and her party had acted in self-defense.

"You realize once these two lawyer up we may be back," the senior inspector warned.

"Ironically, you can find me at an arraignment at the federal courthouse at nine tomorrow morning," she said sourly.

They made a couple of rude comments about criminal defense attorneys as they left. Harri let their smartass remarks pass. With all the negative press Ultramegaperson was getting, they didn't need Harri making the situation worse.

Hours later, Harri and her team hauled their luggage up to their new suite. It was only an hour time difference between Canyon Pointe and San Francisco, but even Steve was dragging as late as it was.

The last thing Harri wanted to do was wake Aisha. Mitch wasn't sleeping through the entire night yet, and her partner needed every little bit of rest she could get. Superpowers did not compensate for sleep depravation.

Harri flopped on the couch while Tim retreated to their bedroom and Steve checked out the view from the balcony. She dialed Aisha's number, but it was Patty who answered after the first ring.

"Aisha Franklin's answering service. May I take a message?"

"Quit messing around, Patty," Harri snapped. "I need to talk to Aisha right now. This is firm business."

"She's not here," Patty answered coolly. "I'll let her know you called—"

There was some scuffling sounds, a few curses, and then Susan's voice.

"Harri, is this about Ultramegaperson's case?"

"Maybe," Harri said. A little guilt danced in the back of her head. She and Aisha had been best friends for so long she inadvertently cut Susan out of a lot of things. She needed to do better when dealing with their new partner. They literally could not afford to lose her.

Harri inhaled sharply. "A couple of goons broke into our hotel rooms. The police just took them away. The fact that it happened so soon after the U.S. attorney general tried to blackmail me gives me the heebie jeebies."

"Are you guys okay?"

"Yeah." Harri relayed the events of the evening.

When she finished, Susan muttered some things that would have made Samuel L. Jackson blush. "This all can't be a coincidence."

"No shit. Two weird incidents—"

"No, three." Susan exhaled loudly. "Sorry to be the bearer of more bad news, but Aisha and Mitch were kidnapped tonight."

CHAPTER 16

Aisha stared at Doctor Liquidation and didn't take the proffered hand. "I've already gone through this with your minions on the ride here. How many times do I have to say the original Ghost Owl is dead before any of you believe me?"

"No body, no death."

Aisha resisted the urge to groan aloud. Instead, she walked over to the loveseat that matched the couch Doctor Liquidation had been sitting on when her minions escorted Aisha into the family room. The supervillain definitely had a thing for blue. The cotton twill upholstery matched the shade of her hair. Aisha set the infant carrier next to her on the floor and sighed as the furniture cradled her abused buttocks.

"Look, I can't deliver the original Ghost Owl to you—"

"But Ghost Owl II can," Doctor Liquidation asserted. She crossed her arms and frowned at Aisha. So did the brunette major domo who had escorted Aisha into the family room.

Mitch started fussing. From the ache in Aisha's breasts, she couldn't wait, not without having the front of her shirt soaking wet. The timing of this kidnapping could not be worse.

"I need to feed my son," she snapped. "So unless you want milk all over your damn upholstery, I'd like those baby supplies I was promised now. We can discuss this Ghost Owl crap while he eats."

Doctor Liquidation nodded to the minion Aisha was pretty certain was Goon Number Two. The goon trotted out of the room.

Goon Number Two came back, this time without the hood or the voice modulator. She was a young white woman, probably about Molly Reinhold's age. Her blond hair was a little disarrayed from the hood she'd been wearing, but she had the same tight bun as Liquidation's major domo, AKA Goon Number Three. Or was that Goon Number Four if the driver was Three. However, Goon Number Two carried a laundry basket full of baby supplies.

"I already washed and sanitized everything, Ms. Franklin," she said in a perky voice that reminded Aisha too much of Molly. "And we have a pet-free environment for your baby."

"Thank you." Aisha quickly changed Mitch's damp diaper before she selected a striped burping towel from the collection. Other than threatening to shoot Rey, neither the supervillain or her minions had made any attempt to harm her or Mitch. If this was related to Ultramegaperson, she needed to learn as much information as she could.

As much as Aisha hated to do this in front of anybody, much less a supervillain she was trying to negotiate with, she unbuttoned her shirt and unhooked the left side of her nursing bra. The brunette major domo's mouth formed a moue of distaste, but tough cookies. They'd put Aisha in this position, so she wasn't going to feel real bad about it. As soon as Mitch latched on and was sucking away, she eyed Doctor Liquidation.

"Let's start with a more pressing matter," Aisha said. "What the hell happened at the Federal Reserve Building in San Francisco this morning? It was all over the news you were duking it out with Ultramegaperson."

Pink flushed Doctor Liquidation's pale cheeks. "That was the other reason I wanted to speak with you. Your firm represents Ultramegaperson, correct?"

"Yes, and?" Aisha prompted.

"I think my employer is trying to set up both me and Ultramegaperson." Doctor Liquidation strode back to the spot on the couch where she perched before and sat down in a cross-legged pose. "They wanted me to steal samples of a new security transmitter for bank dye packs. They were also supposed to provide a distraction for Ultramegaperson to keep them out of the city while my crew performed our job."

Something cold and slimy crawled up Aisha's spine. She needed to confirm with Harri how Ultramegaperson learned about Doctor Liquidation's attempted theft. Someone with access to the superhero alert system had lured Rey into the desert last year in order for Professor Paranoia to abduct him and put a brainwashed Steve in his place.

"I still don't get why you would need the original Ghost Owl."

"Because if this was a con to blame Ultramegaperson for the deaths at the Golden Gate Bridge, my employer needs me and my crew out of the way for it to succeed."

Aisha couldn't fault the supervillain's logic.

"Do you have the transmitters?" Aisha asked.

"Yes." Suspicion flared in Doctor Liquidation's blue eyes.

"Would you be willing to cooperate with law enforcement to nab your employer?"

"Maybe," the supervillain said tentatively. "It depends on whether I have legal representation."

Aisha cocked her head. "As in, you want me to refer you to someone who specializes in supervillain criminal defense?"

"No, I want you to represent me," Doctor Liquidation said.

"Me?" Aisha took advantage of switching Mitch to her right breast to think about the supervillain's request. "That would be a conflict of interest since we already represent Ultramegaperson."

"We're both the victims of the same asshole who wanted to kill all those people on the bridge." Doctor Liquidation waved her right hand. "Besides, once you clear Ultramegaperson, then law enforcement will try to pin those deaths on me. I'm a lot of things, Ms. Franklin, but I've never killed someone!"

"Look, I understand where you're coming from, and I do sympathize with your position." Aisha shook her head. "However, even if I agreed to represent you, all the partners in our firm have a say, and one of our main rules is we don't represent supervillains."

"We also both know that's a lie." Doctor Liquidation scowled at Aisha. "Your firm represents Miss Purrception."

Aisha sighed. "That was a special situation. She agreed to turn herself in if we set up a Christmas reunion with her family. Are you willing to turn yourself in for stealing the new transmitters?"

Doctor Liquidation's jaw worked a few times before she said, "This is why I wanted to speak with the original Ghost Owl. He'd be willing to help me in exchange for returning the transmitters."

Aisha couldn't stop the chuckle that rolled out of her chest. "Oh, honey, you did not know the original Ghost Owl at all if you believe that."

"So he is alive!"

"No, he's not," Aisha murmured. "But the new Ghost Owl is a client. I can relay your message to them. They'd agree to meet with you if you release me and my son unharmed."

"I can't convince you Ultramegaperson and I are on the same side this time?" Bone shone white in Doctor Liquidation's knuckles as her hands curled around her knees. This whole messed-up situation was causing a ton of strain on the woman.

"It's not me you have to convince, Doctor," Aisha said. "There's Ghost Owl II and my partners. Both of which will be difficult to do while I'm your prisoner."

Mitch yawned and snuggled deeper in Aisha's arm. From his lip-smacking, he was already drifting off into his post-meal nap. She wiped drool and milk off both of them and refastened her clothing before she eyed Doctor Liquidation again.

"So what's your decision?" Aisha said.

"All right." Doctor Liquidation blew out a deep breath. "But if this means someone's arrested, then it's just me. Not my girls." She waved at the two goons still in the room.

"I'll relay all your information and wishes to the new Ghost Owl and my partners." Aisha nodded firmly.

She just hoped one of Doctor Liquidation's goons didn't decide her loyalty to her boss was more important than the deal her boss cut. Aisha had no doubt neither she nor Mitch would survive a point-blank plasma burst somewhere in the desert.

CHAPTER 17

"What do you mean Aisha and Mitch were kidnapped?" Harri roared. Tim and Steve in various states of undress raced back to the suite's living room.

"Some jerks with plasma weapons in a white van took the pair as Rey was walking them home from Marta's tonight." Susan sounded far too calm. "We've already tracked them to a place in the western foothills. Rey managed to plant his phone on Aisha before the bad guys forced her into the van."

"Put it on speaker," Tim said. Fear and anger shone on his face. He'd already lived this nightmare. As much as Harri wanted to protect him, she couldn't hide anything from him. Not when his expertise may be necessary to rescue her best friend and her godson.

Harri tapped the icon for the appropriate function. "Susan, Tim and Steve are with me."

"You guys need to stop worrying," Susan said. "Rey's being smart and only watching the place while he's waiting for backup. Sparx is en route since she can get there the quickest. So far, Doctor Liquidation is just talking to Aisha while she feeds Mitch in the family room of the house in the mountains where they're keeping her and the baby."

"Whoa!" Tim moved closer to Harri. "What do you mean Aisha's just talking to Doctor Liquidation?"

"Exactly what I said." Susan was starting to sound a little testy. "Rey's right outside the house. He can see and hear what's happening inside, plus Arthur's recording everything through Rey's phone planted on Aisha. Doctor Liquidation claims the person who hired her to break into the Federal Reserve is setting up both her and Ultramegaperson."

"This is one situation where Rey and Aisha shouldn't have worried about outing themselves," Steve snapped. "Letting a supervillain take Mitch—"

"Get off your high horse," Susan bit back. "They didn't want to risk the baby getting vaporized. You didn't see what one of those plasma bolts did to the exterior brick of the frame shop between here and Marta's."

Susan abruptly softened her tone. "How did things go with Ultramegaperson at Alcatraz?"

"Not good." Harri laid out the events of the day, including the attack at the hotel.

"Too much is happening for these not to be coincidences," Susan murmured. "And before you see the invoice, we needed to bring in a specialty cleaner." She related the details concerning the protests and the blood thrown on Black Falcon and Nix and reassured everyone the two superheroes were both fine.

Harri rubbed her forehead. "For once, I wish Corvus was still running around so I'd know who to blame."

"You knew it was a possibility we didn't root out all of them," Susan said.

"What is that supposed to mean?" Tim growled.

"That wasn't a slam on you or your abilities, Tim," Susan said.

"Someone in the government had to be covering for Trubble for him to be operating Corvus for decades. Someone so deeply entrenched they were careful not to make obvious connections between them and Corvus. Wasn't the NSB alert system used to capture Rey last year?"

Harri met Tim's gaze. His worried expression matched how she felt.

"So you're saying this is like a fire ants' nest?" Harri murmured.

"Yep," Susan said. "You only see the top couple of inches, but those suckers can go several feet into the soil."

"And then they all boil up and bite you." Harri shivered. She'd accidentally stepped on a fire ant nest when she was in kindergarten. Their bites hurt so bad she had lain awake all night, crying.

"These may only be the first couple of bites," Susan said. In the background, Harri could hear voices murmuring before Susan said, "Wait a sec, Harri."

She tapped her foot impatiently. Waiting was certainly not her strong suit.

"Aisha and Mitch will be okay," Steve said assuredly.

"And what gives you that expert opinion?" Harri snapped.

"This is the woman who beat me over the head with a tree to save her husband." A rueful smile filled Steve's face. "What do you think she will do to save her son?"

The kid had a point. However, Harri didn't want to see her best friend go to jail for murder if she had to save Mitch from a supervillain and her minions. Aisha had wanted a baby for so long. The doctors said she'd never be able to conceive again after an ectopic pregnancy nearly killed her. Little Mitch was a freaking miracle on so many levels.

"Harri?" Susan's voice interrupted the maudlin train of thought.

Harri cleared her throat. "We're still here."

"Rey reports that one of the minions is leaving with Aisha and Mitch."

"In the same van?" Tim asked.

"Nope, a sports car this time." Susan murmured something to someone with her before she returned to the phone conversation. "Aisha's cut a deal with Doctor Liquidation for her to meet with the new Ghost Owl. She wants the Owl to help her clear her name in regard to the Golden Gate incident."

"But I'm not in Canyon Pointe—" Tim stopped and turned beet red. "Retirement sucks."

Steve laughed. "You can commiserate with Sparx. She is going to bitch up a storm because she was dragged out of bed for nothing tonight."

"I don't know if Liquidation and the Owl meeting is such a good idea," Harri said.

"If Mitch is out of the firing line, Aisha can bring in Doctor Liquidation." Susan hesitated for a second. "Or the firm could take on representing Doctor Liquidation."

"I thought we all agreed Miss Purrception was a one time thing," Harri said.

"Technically, I wasn't a partner at the time *you* decided to represent her," Susan pointed out. "But if taking on Doctor Liquidation's legal representation is the only way we can clear Ultramegaperson, then we should do it."

"What about conflict of interest?" Harri shouted. It was the only way to release the pounding behind her eyeballs.

"What about the rest of the Reinhold family?" Susan shot back.

Harri really wanted to kick something. Or someone. When Aisha or Jeremy pointed out Harri was wrong, they were a little nicer about it. How had her best friends held their temper in all this years? Not to mention, if Harri and Aisha were constantly skirting the ethics line, how could they expect Susan to refrain?

"All right." Harri inhaled and blew out a deep breath. "I get the message. If you and Aisha can figure out a way to pull this off, I'm behind you."

"So if we can't, you're disavowing us?" Susan's teasing tone was back.

"It'll be a little hard to if we're all sitting in a jail cell together for harboring a fugitive," Harri said sourly. "Any chance you two will have something concrete for me before Ultramegaperson's arraignment in the morning?"

"We'll try," Susan said. "But don't count on it."

"All right." Harri rubbed her forehead. Her headache was getting worse, and she needed to be bright-eyed and conscious at the hearing. "If you can get me anything before ten a.m. your time, great. If not, I'll call once I'm out of court."

"Break a leg," Susan said.

"We've broken enough bones around the office, thank you very much," Tim retorted.

Susan's laughter rang through the receiver before she ended the call.

Harri's thumb hovered over the icon for Rey's number, but calling Aisha now would be a thoroughly stupid move. Especially if her friend and partner was handling the situation with Doctor Liquidation.

"Penny for your thoughts," Steve said, echoing her statement earlier tonight.

"I'm micromanaging again." She set her phone on the end table and scrubbed her hands over her face. "I'm so used to having to ride herd on the staff at the City Attorney's office, I sometimes forget Aisha and Susan are just as capable and experienced as I am."

"Is cutting a deal with Doctor Liquidation such a good idea?" Tim crossed his arms.

Harri matched his stance. "Did you bang her on a rooftop, too?"

"Whoa!" Steve grinned. "So it's true? Miss Purrfection is your ex?"

"That's not the issue," Tim replied through clenched teeth. "And I didn't think the girls should have represented Miss Purrfection either."

"Girls?" Harri stared.

Even Steve winced. "Bad choice of words, dude."

"That's not what I meant!" Tim threw his arms up in the air.

Steve pivoted and stalked toward his room.

"Where are you going?" Harri barked.

He whirled to face her and Tim. "I learned a long time ago that when Mom and Dad fight, it's best not to be in the room." He stomped into his bedroom and slammed the door.

Harri stared at Tim. "Did he just call us Mom and Dad?"

"Well, he does take after your side of the family when it comes to temper tantrums," Tim said.

"Uh-uh." Harri waggled her index finger. "He gets his stubbornness from your side."

Tim stared at the ceiling a moment before he exhaled and looked at her again. "I can fly back to Canyon Pointe tonight."

She shook her head. "Even with light traffic and a cabbie with a lead foot, you won't make the last flight. You need to trust that you trained Rey and Arthur right."

Tim's right eyebrow rose. "Are you saying you don't want to go back right now?"

"Yeah, I do, but I'm a control freak." She shrugged. "All I will accomplish is piss off Aisha. And I trust her more than I trust you."

"Gee, thanks." He waited a beat before he added, "Mom."

"Timothy Mitchell Canyon, I have one hell of a headache, and I don't need your shit right now." Harri jabbed her index finger in the direction of their bedroom. "Now, go to your room before I spank you."

He grinned. "Promise?"

She laughed at his lascivious leer and shook her head. "You do know my intern can hear everything you say."

"Then he'd better be putting on his noise-canceling headphones because Mom and Dad are going to have some make-up sex so you're relaxed for tomorrow's arraignment."

CHAPTER 18

Aisha breathed a sigh of relief when Harper, aka Goon Number Two, turned onto the highway back to Canyon Pointe. Doctor Liquidation's sports car was way more comfortable than her decrepit van, except for Rey's phone digging into her lower vertebrae. Plus, the supervillain and her minions had the correct base for Mitch's infant carrier, so now he lay safely cuddled and sound asleep in the back seat.

"Harper, why do you work for Doctor Liquidation?" Aisha asked softly.

The girl glanced at Aisha before returning her attention to the road. "Because she gave a shit about me."

"Are you a super?"

"No." Tension bled into Harper's voice. "And quit acting like you give a shit."

"What makes you think I don't?"

"Because you sound just like every social worker I ever encountered," Harper bit out.

Aisha chuckled and stretched out her legs. "Well, this is the first time I've ever been accused of acting like a social worker."

"And why is it so funny?" Harper snapped.

"Because my two closest friends were caught in the system until my parents intervened."

"Oh." Harper was silent for a mile before she asked, "Were their parents into drugs?"

"Harri's were. They didn't OD though. They drove their car over a cliff while they were higher than kites." Aisha sighed. Their funeral so soon after Grandma Harri's had done a number on her partner. "Jeremy's parents kicked him out when they found out he was gay."

"Did either of them get pimped out for drugs?" Harper said bitterly.

"No," Aisha admitted. "If Liquidation got you out of that life, she did a good thing."

Harper was quiet for another two miles before she said, "Do you think the new Ghost Owl could talk the doctor into going straight like he did?"

"I don't know. Maybe." Aisha considered the girl's wording. "What do you hope to accomplish by convincing Doctor Liquidation to give up being a supervillain?"

"She would make an awesome, kickass superhero if she could see the financial advantage." Harper glanced at Aisha again. "I read a *Forbes* article on what Eagle Forever and Captain Justice's estates alone are pulling in, and they're both dead. Imagine what the doctor could do on licensing while she's still alive."

Aisha laughed. "Sounds like you already have this planned out."

"Well, if the new Ghost Owl can go straight after his predecessor's legacy as a vigilante, why can't Doctor Liquidation become a superhero? I mean, how difficult would it be?"

"It would really depend on her outstanding charges and warrants," Aisha cautioned.

"Are you really considering taking her on as a client?" Harper practically quivered with excitement. "I mean, I know we'd have to do a total makeover. Change her moniker. All the jazz she'd need to do to go legit."

"That's a lot of jazz you're asking for," Aisha said. "And there's no guarantee she'd agree to it."

"If the Ghost Owl helps her clear her name, she would," Harper said firmly.

"First, I need to see if the new Ghost Owl will agree to the meeting," Aisha replied.

She hated lying to Harper, but it was only temporarily. She'd had already decided. If Harri could rehabilitate Professor Venom and turn him into a productive citizen and a family man, then she could do the same for Doctor Liquidation.

She hoped anyway.

If she didn't get herself killed in the process.

CHAPTER 19

The obnoxious light and ringing of Harri's phone woke her out of a sound sleep. She automatically reached for it, thumbed the answer icon, and snapped, "What?"

"Harri, it's Gil Wilcrest."

That statement jolted her out of her half-conscious state, and she sat up. "Gil, what's wrong?"

"Some motherfucking asshole set my house on fire!"

"Are you okay?" The shouting and sirens in the background registered thanks to the adrenaline pumping through her veins. The cursing didn't shock her. Grandma Harri had said far worse whenever the subject of the Canyon family came up.

Speaking of the Canyon family, Tim rolled over and blearily asked, "What's going on now?"

"I'm fine. Dougal is fine. But I don't have a damn thing to wear for court tomorrow, Harri." The elderly attorney sounded more angry than upset, which was weird.

"I'm coming to pick you up, Gil." Harri flung back the covers and felt around for her underwear in the dark hotel room. "You and Dougal—wait. Who is Dougal?"

"My dog, Harri." Gil huffed. "And no hotel is going to take a dog. Not to mention, I have no clothes."

Harri closed her eyes and gathered some patience. "Please, tell me you were wearing pajamas when you and Dougal evacuated the house."

"Well, of course, I was," Gil snapped. "What kind of man do you think I am?"

The light of her phone outlined Tim's totally naked form. So much for his little interlude of relaxing her. Harri rubbed her eyes and returned her attention to the conversation.

"I wasn't impugning your manners," Harri said. "I just wanted to know if I needed to bring something with me for you to wear."

There was a long moment before Gil said, "I'm sorry for snapping at you. It's been a long time since I was a target because of a case I took on, and all the friends I would have normally called are either dead or in a retirement home."

"You think this is because of Ultramegaperson?"

Gil snorted. "The bastards tried to make me look like a doddering old fool who left the goddam stove gas on. As I pointed out to the fire chief, I ate out tonight with a fellow attorney, and I sure as hell didn't smell any gas when I returned home. At least, back in the fifties and sixties, the FBI boys got a little more creative."

Harri reached over and turned on the bedside lamp. "Gil, what's your home address?" She wrote down the street and number he gave her. "I'll be there as soon as I can."

"What happened to Gil?" Tim sat up at the same time there was a knock on the bedroom door.

"Give me a sec, Steve. I only want to have to tell this story once." She grabbed her underwear, which was located under Tim's ankle, and shimmied into them on her way to her suitcase. She pulled on a t-shirt and a pair of jeans. It wasn't worth bothering with a bra this late at night. She glanced at the alarm clock on the night stand on Tim's side of the bed.

Or this early in the morning either.

"Okay, Steve, I'm decent."

He opened the door and peered around the edge.

"Come on in." Harri dug socks out of her suitcase and sat at the foot of the king-size bed to put them on.

Steve stepped into the bedroom. At least, he was dressed this time. "What happened to Gil?"

"Someone tried to kill him." She slipped on her left athletic shoe and tied it. "Arson via his gas stove."

"He's damn lucky his house didn't blow up," Tim muttered. "Let me get dressed."

"No," Harri and Steve said at the same time.

"We're both dressed," Harri said.

"And Gil can have my bed," Steve added.

"You both have to be at court tomorrow," Tim protested.

"Get some sleep, honey." Harri reached over and patted his leg. "We'll be back as soon as we can." She grabbed the SUV keys and her phone and raced out of the bedroom before he could protest further. Steve followed and closed the door behind him.

"You've got your keycard?" She looked up at her intern as she slung her purse over her shoulder.

"Yes." Steve frowned. "Don't you have yours?"

"I do." She charged out of the suite and headed for the elevator. Once again, Steve followed and closed the door.

"And?" His right eyebrow rose. For an instant, she would have sworn his brother Rey was looking at her.

"If we get into trouble, I want you to fly Gil back here," she murmured.

"You think Susan is right," Steve said as the elevator doors parted. "That this is another fire ant bite."

"Yep." Harri jabbed the button for the lobby. "I just pray we don't get bitten again befor the arraignment today."

Traffic was fairly busy with the first early morning commuters when Harri and Steve pulled onto Gil's street. Thankfully, his house wasn't far from their hotel. She would have liked to visit the neighborhood in the daytime. Quaint Victorian-style houses guarded the narrow street. A police officer directing traffic motioned for her to turn right. She rolled down the vehicle's driver side window.

"Ma'am," he yelled over the noise coming from the fire engines. "You can't come this way. We've got a two-alarm blaze."

"I know," Harri shouted back. "It's my friend Gil's house. He called me because he doesn't have any family in the city."

The officer hesitated, then made his decision. "Pull in right behind my squad car and park. I can't let your vehicle get in the fire department's way." He leaned his head over his shoulder and spoke into his radio.

Harri carefully parallel parked behind the police car. She and Steve jumped out of their rental vehicle and headed up the street. They found Gil sitting in the bay of an ambulance. He was surrounded by a paramedic, a cop, and a couple of people in pajamas. The dark-haired and very young paramedic was trying to take Gil's vitals, but the elderly attorney kept batting at the paramedic's blue-gloved hands. More neighbors in their night clothes shivered on the sidewalks as they watched the fire department put out the blaze.

"Gil!" Harri rushed toward the elderly attorney.

The cop turned to look at her.

Of course, it had to be Officer Bishop at the scene.

"Well, well, well." Her teeth appeared to flicker from red to blue and back again from emergency vehicle lights. "If it isn't Taser girl. You've had one hell of a night."

The two people in bathrobes stepped aside so Harri could approach. Neither of them looked that much younger than Gil.

"No kidding." Harri answered the cop before she turned to Gil. "Are you sure you're okay?"

"More pissed off than anything," he said. Something white moved underneath the silvery thermal blanket wrapped around him. A little head with shiny black eyes poked out from between the folds. The dog barked once.

"Now, Dougal, be nice," Gil chided.

Harri held out her palm for the West Highland terrier to sniff. She'd thought about getting a dog when she still had her townhouse, but her obscene work hours wouldn't have been fair to any canine. And once she moved into her loft at the Lechuza Building, she had no yard for a dog to play in.

Dougal thoroughly inspected her hand, then gave it a quick lick. Harri crouched next to Gil and scratched Dougal under his chin.

"I'm sorry I don't have any treats for you, little guy," she murmured.

"Well, shit." Gil looked on the edge of crying. Ash and dirt clung to his gnomish beard. "Lost his dog food, his toys, and all our medicines, too."

Crap. This was supposed to be a business trip, not a rescue. But she couldn't leave the elderly man alone, even if he wasn't her co-counsel.

"We've got a room for you at our hotel," Harri assured him.

"Oh, pshaw. There's no reason for him to go to a hotel." The elderly woman elbowed the man standing with her. "Gil can stay with us, can't he, Alfred?"

"Sure," Alfred said amicably.

"I appreciate the offer, Mabel," Gil said kindly. "But Harri and I have to be in court in the morning. And I don't think Alfred's clothes will fit me."

The conversation distracted Gil enough the poor paramedic could finally check the elderly attorney's vital signs.

"Ms. Winters?"

She looked up at Bishop.

"There's a twenty-four-hour market." The police officer rattled off the directions and address. "They'll have toiletries and kibble to get you through the rest of the night."

"But they don't have any clothes," Gil grumbled.

"No." Bishop shook her head. "Unfortunately, you're not going to find anything reasonably priced downtown—"

"Wait." Harri straightened. "Isn't there a Winters Department Store still on Market Street?"

"Yeah, but they're expensive as hell—" Bishop blinked. "Wait a minute. You're one of those Winters?"

Harri shrugged. "Well, the family doesn't own the chain any more, but I think I still have enough pull I can call a personal shopper for Gil first thing in the morning."

"That's why your name sounded so familiar!" Gil's face lit up, and Dougal barked a couple of times at his human's excitement. "I met your grandmother at Eagle Forever's annual charity auction. Oh dear, I guess it's been nearly fifty years ago."

Harri chuckled to hide her discomfort. "I sincerely apologize for whatever she did to you half a century ago."

"My dear, she had been donating anonymously for years to the Superhero Legal Defense Fund!" Gil exclaimed. "She and Eagle Forever are the reason I was able to help all those poor souls who found themselves on the wrong side of frivolous lawsuits."

"You can tell me all about it on the ride back to the hotel, Gil." Harri looked at the paramedic. "Assuming we don't need to make a side trip to the ER?"

The paramedic shook his head. "His lungs are clear, but he should follow up with his general practioner in the morning."

"I will. I will." Gil shot Harri a cross look. "After I get some clothes and deal with our case."

"It's a little bit of a walk to where we're parked, Mr. Wilcrest," Steve said. "You want to take my arm?"

"I can walk just fine," Gil grumbled, but when he stood, he wobbled and nearly dropped his dog.

"Here, let me carry Dougal, and you take Steve's arm." When Gil opened his mouth to protest, Harri waggled her right index finger at him. "You give me any lip, and I'll tell Steve to carry you."

Gil scowled at her, but he grudgingly turned over Dougal to her. The small white dog didn't argue. Gil took Steve's proffered arm.

"Don't worry, Gil," Alfred assured him. "Mabel and I will keep an eye on your place until you get back."

"And we'll call Billy to come over with his boys and board up the place for you once the fire department is sure the fire is out," Mabel added.

"Thanks." Gil bobbed his head. "I appreciate your help."

Together, Harri, Gil, and Steve headed down the street. Steve did his best to keep the elderly attorney upright without being too obvious. Dougal whimpered a little bit before he snuggled as deep as he could in Harri's arms. She couldn't blame him. The air was chilly, and fog seemed to roll up the street like soft misty kittens around their ankles. It made Harri glad she'd put on her socks.

Gil seemed to forget about Grandma Harri as Steve executed a J-turn and drove toward the little market Officer Bishop mentioned. As the SUV pulled in front of the market, soft snores from both Gil and Dougal came from the back seat.

While Steve ran in to fetch the toiletries, Harri tried to relax. But Gil's mention of Eagle Forever gnawed on her brain. The retired superhero had been killed when Seismic Shift "accidentally" destroyed the Lake County Retirement Home a year and a half ago.

After their tussle with Seismic Shift and exposing the so-called hero's illegal activities, both she and Aisha suspected Forever Eagle's death wasn't so accidental after all. But with all the chaos Corvus had been sowing in their own lives, they hadn't followed up on the matter.

And though Grandma Harri never hid her penchant for social justice, she also never mentioned she knew any supers. Whenever the subject had come up, Grandma Harri merely sniffed in disdain and made some comment about how uncouth the supers were by running or flying about in skintight costumes. So why would she support the Superhero Legal Defense Fund?

Once they cleared Ultramegaperson's name, Harri needed to take a serious look at all the connections between her grandmother, Forever Eagle, and retired general Byron S. Trubble because something about this whole mess smelled to high heaven.

CHAPTER 20

Aisha waited until Harper pulled away from the curb in Doctor Liquidation's sports car before she approached the garage side door into the building. She nearly jumped out of her skin when Qiang in her Sparx gear stepped from behind a nearby pillar in the Lechuza Building's parking garage.

"A little warning next time," Aisha hissed so as not to wake up Mitch.

"I'm not the one who got herself snatched from the sidewalk, and then played tea party with a supervillain," Qiang growled back.

"Both of you need to stop fighting." Rey, also dressed in his superhero persona Black Falcon, landed next to the women. "Let's get the baby in bed first, then we can argue about Doctor Liquidation."

Arthur had designed a face shield for Black Falcon similar to Tim's original version for the Ghost Owl. It made sense for him to have the full face cover since he learned he had an identical twin brother who did not want to enter the superhero arena. With Rey's face totally covered, Aisha wasn't sure if he was angry with her, angry with Qiang, or angry with Doctor Liquidation.

If Aisha had to make a bet, she would place her money on all three.

No one said anything while the antique elevator wheezed its way up the shaft. The fact that Arthur hadn't buzzed her via the intercom when she unlocked the door meant he was watching them on the cameras.

Or else he, Rey, and Qiang already spoke via comms before the two superheroes showed up in the garage.

The elevator groaned to a stop at the fourth floor. Arthur, Susan, and Miguel Esperanza, their building manager and former sidekick to the original Ghost Owl, climbed on board the car. Still, no one said anything.

So that's the way it was going to be, huh? Aisha clenched her jaw to keep from screaming at the crew and waking Mitch. Dammit! She and her infant son were the ones who were kidnapped tonight.

The elevator whined to a stop at the fifth floor, and Aisha pushed past Arthur and Miguel to get out of the tight space. She stalked down the hallway and jabbed the buttons on the lock to her loft. The security device hummed, and she was about to jerk the door open when Rey grabbed her hand and slid up his face plate. His gold eyes stared at her, except it wasn't truly anger than shone from them. More like concern.

"Are you angry I didn't stop Doctor Liquidation's minion after dinner?" he murmured.

"What?" Aisha said the word a little too loudly. Mitch stirred in his infant carrier. She also noticed the rest of the group hung back beside the elevator.

"No," she said more quietly. "I thought you were angry with me for motioning you to back off. I was afraid those plasma rifles of theirs would hurt you or kill Mitch."

The whisper of a smile tilted Rey's lips ever so slightly. "I thought we were doing better at communicating. I guess we still need to work on it. I also didn't want you to rip off the loft door accidentally."

"I wasn't going to—" she started.

"Baby, when you go silent, you're so angry you sometimes forget you have superstrength."

Aisha relaxed her grip on the door handle. It sucked he was right. They'd already replaced the refrigerator after she accidentally ripped its door off the hinges thanks to her irritation after a particularly nasty arbitration with a flooring company who'd used Cobblestone's likeness without his permission in a totally derogatory manner.

The rest of their little group quietly approached them as Rey rolled open the loft door.

"He's right you know." Leave it to Arthur to say what everyone else was probably thinking. "About forgetting you're superstrong now."

"Would you prefer me yelling like Harri?" Aisha said.

"Oh, please, no," Arthur said fervently. "She's scary when she yells."

"Let me put Mitch to bed," she said. "Then we'll talk."

Everyone filled Aisha in on the events after Doctor Liquidation's minions drove off with her and Mitch, including the phone call with Harri about the attack on her team in San Francisco. When they finished, Aisha muttered, "Screw the ban on alcohol while nursing. I'm getting wine."

"May I have a glass, too?" Susan asked.

Rey ran back to their bedroom and changed clothes while Susan helped Aisha by retrieving soft drinks and water from the new refrigerator for everyone else. Once everyone was seated in the space in the loft designated as the living room, Aisha said, "I'm heading back to meet with Doctor Liquidation tonight as the Ghost Owl."

"What?" Susan exclaimed. "Why?"

Rey and Qiang merely exchanged looks before they said in unison, "Not without backup."

"Because, for whatever reason, she thinks the Ghost Owl can help her clear her name regarding the destruction of the Golden Gate Bridge," Aisha said.

"If you're going to be flying tonight, maybe you should lay off the wine," Miguel said. Aisha shot him a dirty look. She only poured a quarter of a glass, half her usual amount before her unexpected pregnancy.

"Screw the wine," Susan snapped. "There is no reason for you to go back out there tonight. You got lucky. Nothing happened to you or the baby. You don't know if Liquidation is telling the truth. It could be a set up to kill the Owl."

"What could she do to me?" Aisha pointed out. "I'm damn near invulnerable."

"She could drown you," Arthur said softly. He stared at the floor.

"He has a point." Rey twined his fingers between the fingers of Aisha's free hand. "Despite all our abilities, we still need to breathe."

"Which is why you shouldn't go back there in your super persona without backup," Qiang said firmly.

"Not to mention, someone tried to kill your law partner tonight," Miguel added. "We have no idea what is really going on."

"Corvus could have rebuilt itself." Susan waved her free hand. "They don't like you, Harri, or the Ghost Owl. They blame the three of you for their exposure and downfall. And I don't want to run this firm by myself."

"All right. All right." Aisha swallowed the rest of her glass. "Qiang, you're coming with me. Rey, you're on baby duty. Arthur, you're our handler. Miguel and Susan, get some freaking sleep."

Arthur, Miguel, and Susan headed out the loft door. Qiang stayed in the rocking chair with a scowl marring her face. Rey followed Aisha back to their bedroom and leaned against the doorjamb.

"What?" she said as she kicked off her shoes.

"I get why you don't want me to go—" he started.

"Do you really?" she snapped.

"You don't want Mitch to lose both parents if you're wrong," he said.

Her eyes watered with the emotions she'd clamped down all night. "No, I can't handle losing you again."

"We've never really talked about last year, have we?" He crossed their bedroom and sat next to her.

"No." She swallowed the lump in her throat and swiped at the wetness threatening to spill down her cheeks. "Tonight brought all of that fear back. When that goon pointed the plasma rifle at you—"

Rey pulled her into his arms. "I do understand. I had the same terrible fear I would lose you the night Corvus chased us in your car across the city. And again, tonight, when that van drove away."

Aisha relaxed against his chest. "I wouldn't go at all if I believed Doctor Liquidation was lying. The problem is she's adamant the original Ghost Owl is still alive, and she wants to meet with him."

"Well, Miss Purrception did *know* the original Ghost Owl." Laughter rumbled through Rey. "Maybe there's a reason Doctor Liquidation is so adamant."

"Oh, my god." Aisha laughed with him. "Whatever you do, do not say that in front of Harri. She would totally kill Tim."

<h1 style="text-align:center">CHAPTER 21</h1>

The sound of the night air whistling past Aisha's helmet and face shield made her giddy. As much trouble as the HRSP had given her in the first trimester, the sheer joy of flying made up for Xquic gifting her with permanent abilities. Part of her wanted to remove the faceplate from her superhero outfit to feel the wind on her face, but that would be a stupid move. Cameras were everywhere these days, even this far out in the desert. She couldn't chance her secret identity being discovered.

Qiang glided beside Aisha in her black and white Sparx outfit, but the other woman's electromagnetic abilities weren't the reason the comms were silent. Plus, Qiang hadn't even argued when Aisha said Qiang was Aisha's backup for tonight, which was weird. Qiang had a solid opinion about everything.

"You could have refused to come," Aisha said.

Qiang snorted. "Mitch doesn't need to lose both parents because his mother is naïve."

"And Connor doesn't need to lose his last parent because she's too stubborn to say no," Aisha responded.

After a long pause, Qiang said, "I came because the house is too quiet."

She had been anxious last year when her son attended a camp that specialized in kids with autism. But Connor's friendship with Miguel's son Javier had helped the kid come out of his shell. Connor had been excited about the event this year instead of overwhelmed.

With her mom in rehab, her father in an assisted living apartment, and Connor at camp, Qiang probably had other plans this week. Plans involving Steve, who was now in San Francisco with Harri and Tim. Qiang's house was the quietest it would have been in years.

"Why don't you come over tomorrow night?" Aisha said. "I'll kick out Rey and Mitch, and we can have a girls' night."

"How about we focus on this mission?" Qiang was quiet for a long moment before she added, "A girls' night would be nice though."

"Okay." Aisha grinned, though it was probably a good thing her face shield hid her expression. Qiang wouldn't hesitate to electrocute her.

A few minutes later, they approached the house where Doctor Liquidation's minions had brought Aisha. Qiang hung back while Aisha swooped down. She spotted Doctor Liquidation and her four minions. The decrepit van they'd used for the kidnapping was in the drive again, and they were loading gear into it.

Aisha carefully dropped to the scrub pines behind the garage. She circled around the building and stepped into the security light illuminating the side of the house. "Leaving so soon?"

The four minions whirled around to face her. None of them had their masks on, and all of them were armed. Like Harper and Liquidation's major domo, the other two were fairly young women. Had the supervillain recruited them all from the streets like she had Harper?

Aisha slowly raised her hands. "Franklin relayed your request, Doctor. If you changed your mind about talking to me, I'll leave quietly."

The supervillain stepped in front of her minions. "Who are you? The original Ghost Owl or the pretender?"

"The original Ghost Owl is dead."

"You're lying," Doctor Liquidation growled.

"If you don't want my help—"

"How'd you get your powers?" the supervillain asked.

"You wouldn't believe me if I told you." Aisha chuckled.

"Try me."

"The Mayan goddess Xquic."

"Why would she do that?" Interesting that Doctor Liquidation didn't question the existence of a pagan goddess. The four minions lowered their weapons, including the dark-haired scowling white girl with magenta streaks in her hair. Aisha suspected Magenta Streaks was the bad-tempered Goon Number One.

Aisha shrugged. "Because the original Jatz'om Kuh died, and her people needed a protector. I also know Franklin told you all of this already."

"Why did you go legit?" Doctor Liquidation shook her head. "He was the greatest of all the supers. He never got caught. Why the hell would you compromise what he stood for?"

"What he stood for was looking out for the little people." Aisha slowly lowered her arms. "And that's what I'm trying to do here."

"You think I'm little?" Outrage filled the supervillain's voice.

"Franklin thinks you're in over your head." Aisha gestured at the van. "What I see is someone in over her head about to run. If your employer knows how to locate you, you're not going to be able to run for long. You showed your good faith earlier by releasing Franklin and her kid. Give me the new bank transmitters and help me clear Ultramegaperson by telling me who your employer is, and I can get Winters &

Franklin to negotiate lesser charges against you and your crew with the federal attorneys office."

Doctor Liquidation drew in a deep breath and released a white puff of air. The tiny cloud quickly dissipated. "All right—"

"No!" The major domo raised her rifle and pointed it at Aisha. "He's trying to trick you. You can't surrender to him."

"Natalie!" Doctor Liquidation snapped. "The Ghost Owl is doing what he's supposed to do, which is asking for my surrender. That's the reason I was trying to get you girls out of here before he arrived."

"Oh, I know no one gives a rat's ass about minions." Natalie sneered. "Give me the transmitters, I'll leave, and then you can negotiate with the Ghost Owl all you want."

"You'd abandon the doctor?" Harper stepped between Natalie and the supervillain. "After everything she's done for us?"

"She used us!" Natalie motioned with her weapon. "Get out of the way, give me the damn transmitters, and I won't hurt you."

"Stop and think about this for a minute—" Harper said.

"You don't get it!" Natalie fidgeted. "The people who hired the doc knew she'd double-cross them! If I don't deliver the transmitters in a couple of hours, we're all dead!"

"Natalie, I can help you," Aisha said as she took a step closer to Harper. Natalie was on the edge. Her finger twitched near the trigger button. Aisha prayed she was fast enough to get Harper out of the way. "I can apprehend these people, and you and everyone else here will be safe."

"They want you dead!" Natalie shrieked. "And they'll let me live if I deliver your body to them!"

Harper stepped closer to her comrade. "You're not a murderer—"

Natalie's index finger pressed the trigger button on her weapon.

A wave of water slammed into Aisha, sweeping her into Harper. Bright green light flashed, and her visor automatically darkened. A horrible scream pierced her ears, followed by another, different cry of pain. Someone grabbed Aisha's arm and hauled her upright.

"You okay?" Sparx's voice sounded worried.

"Yeah," Aisha said. "Harper?"

A groan came from near Aisha's feet. "Anybody get the number of that tank?" Harper's voice immediately switched to a high-pitched wail.

"Night vision," Aisha murmured. Her face plate blinked. Instead of normal spectrum light, everything had a greenish cast. She wished she hadn't switched on that feature. Doctor Liquidation's body was splayed on the ground.

Or what was left of it.

A wave of nausea swept through Aisha when she realized the water on her and the puddle she stood in was part of the supervillain, too. Natalie lay on her back, stunned.

Aisha stalked to the woman, bent over her, and yanked her up by the collar of her odd gear. "Who ordered you to take the transmitters?"

"Back, Owl!" Sparx ordered and the same time Aisha's helmet picked up a radio signal.

Aisha release the woman's collar and jumped backward. Natalie's body convulsed, and there was a distinctive odor of flesh burning. When Natalie stilled, blood oozed from her nostrils, and her eyes stared at nothing.

"What did you do to her?" the woman with magenta stripes in hair shouted.

"It wasn't us," Sparx bit out. "A radio signal triggered something in her body."

In the distance, an engine roared to life. Something snapped deep in Aisha. Two women were dead and a client was in jail. And all over a new design of ink pack transmitters? Well, she'd had enough.

Aisha launched herself skyward, listening for the nearby engine.

"Ghost Owl, get your ass back here!" Sparx yelled through the comm.

Aisha ignored her backup. She arrowed for the sound. Amongst the scrub trees, she spotted an SUV on a dirt track. The vehicle was definitely outfitted for off-roading.

She dove for the vehicle. The back window flipped up. A figure wearing night goggles lifted something on his shoulder. The device flashed.

Too late, she recognized the rocket launcher. She flung herself to the left. The rocket hit her right boot and exploded.

CHAPTER 22

Aisha tumbled through the air until she slammed into something hard enough to knock all air out of her lungs. Her ears rang, and she was certain she was going to puke.

She blinked, but there were only bright spots flashing on her retinas. The explosion must have knocked out her visor's displays and protective apps. She tried to take a tiny breath, but damn, it hurt.

Someone shaking her shoulders was not helping the nausea one bit. She knocked away the hands, but gently. Just in case.

"Dammit, wake up, Owl!" Sparx yelled.

"I am awake!" More quietly, she added, "If you don't stop shaking me, I'm going to puke all over you."

"Sorry."

"The SUV—"

"It's gone," Sparx said angrily. "I knocked over two trees onto the road to try to stop them, but they had the right suspension to go around them. Not to mention, it was a stupid rookie move for you to take off after it by yourself."

Qiang was totally right. Aisha wanted to kick herself. She'd let her temper get the better of her, which was a Harri move. She'd just gotten so damn mad at the senseless deaths of two people.

"Maybe Harri's right." Aisha carefully sat up. Nothing felt broken. "Maybe getting into the super business was a dumb move on my part."

"Harri's not right." Sparx scowled at her. "But you just can't go off half-cocked after the bad guys." She exhaled and gazed in the direction the SUV had been traveling. "There's definitely something going on, and it's much deeper than civilians accidently getting killed in a supers' battle in San Francisco. Someone definitely wanted Natalie dead before she talked to you."

⁂

They flew back to the house Doctor Liquidation and her minions were using. The van and the two bodies were still there. The three surviving minions and the sports car were gone.

Aisha searched the van and the house while Sparx called in the NSB. Deaths meant a mound of paperwork, even though neither Aisha or Qiang were responsible for them. However, Aisha couldn't find the transmitters or anything linking Liquidation to her employers.

When the NSB team arrived, Aisha gave the agent in charge, Wilbur Nesmith, a recording of the encounter on a micro SDHC card. He slipped it into his laptop and watched the footage from Aisha's chest camera. Arthur had merely clipped the section from their approach to the house to where Sparx had yelled at Aisha as she lay on the boulder she'd crushed in her crash landing.

The NSB agent was older than Aisha had expected. Tall, in his sixties at least, with a full head of salt-and-pepper hair. He also had the calm, steady air of a Presbyterian minister. He looked like he'd be more comfortable in a cardigan and reading by the fireplace than trudging around a murder scene.

Agent Nesmith grunted at the end of the video. "Sparx is right. That was a damn stupid rookie move when you don't know who you're up against."

"I'm aware of that, sir," Aisha said. "It won't happen again."

He nodded. "However, I wish more of you supers were wearing chest cameras. This will make my job a little easier. This Aisha Franklin you were discussing, she's one of Ultramegaperson's attorneys of record, too, isn't she?" Agent Nesmith's attention switched from Aisha to Sparx and back again.

"Yes, sir," they said in unison. Sparx added, "Ours, too."

"You might want to pass the word among your friends who use that firm to watch their backs," Nesmith said.

"You think someone's targeting the firm again?" Aisha asked.

"Possibly," the NSB agent rubbed his chin. "Trubble had a lot of friends." He shrugged. "Now that you're out in the open so to speak, it could be a matter of some upstart wanting the privilege of taking down the new Ghost Owl. Look, kid." He waved his hand. "You were smart enough to bring backup. Just don't act stupid again, and you'll be fine."

"What about Ms. Franklin?" Sparx blurted. "Aren't you going to talk to her?"

Agent Nesmith made a show of checking his watch. "How about I do it at a decent hour, Sparx? Why don't you two get some sleep yourselves? I'll contact your attorneys' office if I have anymore questions."

"Yes, sir," Aisha murmured.

Thank you, sir," Sparx added.

The flight home was a hell of a lot quieter than the trip to Doctor Liquidation's hide-out.

"You can stay in our spare bedroom, tonight," Aisha offered when they entered the Canyon Point city limits.

"No thanks, not tonight." Sparx laughed. "But I'm holding you to that girl's night, so I may take you up on it tomorrow night if I have too much wine."

"Okay. Good night." Aisha saluted her before she shot towards the north side of the Canyon Block. She checked for any observers before she landed on the broken concrete of the sidewalk and slipped through a heavy steel door into the abandoned subway stop.

Descending through the unused tunnels was a little eerie. Rats scampered away from her suit lights. Even her enhanced vision couldn't pick up anything in the utter darkness of underground without additional illumination. Thank goodness, she could fly through the underground maze. The thought of her boots in the god-knew-what crap that coated the floors was enough to give her the willies.

Finally, she approached the passageway from the old Canyon Industries headquarters into the basement of the Lechuza Building. She landed and stripped off her gloves in order to place her palm against the lock. The panel flashed and beeped before the thick steel door swung open on well-oiled hinges.

Before she could touch any switches, lights winked on down the corridor, the seen security devices blinked off, and the electric hum of the unseen protective measures went silent. Arthur must have been watching on the security monitors.

Poor guy. He stayed up the entire night so she had support if she needed it. She definitely needed to make it up to their IT manager for inconveniencing him. At least, more than the healthy raise they'd given Arthur last month.

Aisha entered the main computer lab for the Owl's Nest. Sure enough, energy drink cans littered Arthur's desk. He pivoted on his chair and stretched.

"I'm glad you made it home okay."

"Thanks for turning on the lights." The NSB logo on the main screen caught her attention, and she leaned closer to read the text. "Keeping an eye on the government?"

"It seems prudent given the events over the last twenty-four hours," Arthur said.

Aisha straightened, pulled off her helmet, and ran the fingers of her right hand through her curls. "Does Tim know what you're up to?"

"No." Arthur grimaced. It made his overly large nose look even more prominent on his pale face. "I didn't want to bother him. He seemed as close to peace as he could get over his wife and son's deaths with Trubble and the Corvus people in prison."

"So what made you start digging into the NSB?" Aisha said.

"Rey's fake NSB summons last year." It was the closest she'd ever heard real anger come from Arthur. "Plus the dirty trick your former employer played on Susan. Even if certain persons weren't in direct cahoots with Trubble, that doesn't mean they don't have similar aims and means to make trouble for us."

"Wait a minute." Aisha cocked her head. "'Cahoots'?"

"It was a word my grandfather used." Regret passed across Arthur's face.

"You miss him?"

Arthur nodded. "He was the only person who spent time with me as a child. When he died . . ."

It was rare for Arthur to talk about his family. From the little Patty had gotten out of him, his parents weren't actively abusive, but total neglect was its own form of child abuse.

He sighed and turned back to his large monitor. Pushing him wouldn't get Aisha anywhere with their IT expert, and she couldn't afford to lose him.

Not now.

"Anyway, soon after you, as in Aisha Franklin, were released, a call went out on the NSB notification system." Arthur tapped a couple of buttons and the NSB's system log rolled up the screen. "This one right here." He jabbed a finger at a particular line.

"There's no hero code name."

"There's an invisible character on the entry. Not even the system admin can see these records," Arthur added. "I discovered a back door into their network." He scrolled through more records. "Here's the one that set up Rey to be captured."

Despite her fatigue from the insanity of the night, rage boiled through her. "Those bastards. And I can't even use this."

"Not without admitting I illegally hacked their system," Arthur admitted. He looked up at her again.

"And tipping off whoever's piggybacking the system to send out their own messages," she murmured. "Can you see what device tonight's message was sent to?"

"A burner phone that's already been destroyed or deactivated," he answered promptly.

She folded her arms over her chest as she considered the problem. "They needed line of sight to activate whatever was in Natalie's body that killed her."

"The bad guys sent to Doctor Liquidation's cabin may have had a mission other than Natalie's death," Arthur said.

"Yeah, I've noticed how popular the Ghost Owl is all of the sudden," Aisha grumbled.

"Given the government's penchant for stealing supers' children, you may only be the means to get a hold of Mitch."

At Arthur's words, icy fear stabbed Aisha in the heart. She couldn't lose the child she'd dreamt of for so long. She'd die before anything happened to him.

And maybe that's exactly what someone wanted.

CHAPTER 23

Harri rarely capitalized on the Winters name, but for Gil's sake, she pulled some strings. Okay, she pulled a lot of strings. More like she yanked on the strings.

Hard.

Mitzi, the personal shopper, showed up in the hotel lobby at eight a.m. with a selection of clothes in Gil's size. She was taller than Harri, but then, so was nearly everyone. She wore a thin head scarf to keep her dark hair from her face. The scarf matched her 60's-style sleeveless midi dress and brightly colored boots. With her pale, unblemished skin, it was hard to tell her exact age.

She was a little flustered when she first arrived. Probably because Harri had threatened her boss with taking the story of their refusal to help an elderly man whose house burnt down to all the major networks and a few minor ones.

But once in the suite, Mitzi was all business. Gil was quickly decked out in a navy suit with a sky blue and silver tie that brought out his eyes. Steve shook out the brand new dress shirt, and Gil hurried after him to supervise the use of their bathroom's shower to steam the wrinkles from the stiff cotton. Well, Gil went as fast as he could. He limped despite sleeping in Steve's bed.

"Pardon me for asking, but does he need a suit so soon?" Mitzi shook her head as she pulled out matching shoes and socks from her case. "I can pin it and take it back to the store so the suit's a better fit."

"Thanks for the offer, but we have court in—" Harri pulled out her phone to check the time. "—half an hour. Guys! Forget the wrinkles! We need to go!"

"Someone's suing that sweet old man?" Mitzi looked horrified.

"No, he's an attorney." Harri tried not to scream at Steve and Gil again while she slid her phone back into her own suit pocket. They could not afford to be late to this arraignment.

Steve dashed out of the second bedroom at damn near superspeed. Luckily, Mitzi wasn't looking at him until he said, "Where's the socks and shoes?"

"Here." The personal shopper held up the shoe box and a package of dress socks.

Steve snatched them, but he flashed Mitzi a charming smile at the same time to ameliorate his rudeness. She watched him stride back into the second bedroom.

Mitzi turned to Harri and whispered, "Is he taken?"

"Yes. Sorry."

Mitzi giggled. "Does he have a brother?"

"Twin." Harri smiled sympathetically. "Also, taken."

"Damn," Mitzi muttered.

"I think Gil's available," Harri teased.

Mitzi giggled again. "I might just have to ask him out."

"Steve! Gil! Tim!" Harri roared. "The elevator! Now!"

"All of you are leaving? Now?" Mitzi wrung her hands. "But the clothes—"

Tim strode out of their bedroom, his silver gray suit on and his computer bag slung over his shoulder. "Under normal circumstances, we'd let you stay and order room service, but someone tried to kill all four of us last night. Gunmen broke into our previous hotel room, and someone set Gil's house on fire."

"And whoever it was, may come in here and kill you just because you are here." Harri donned her cross body bag and grabbed her legal file. Steve and Gil strode into the suite's living room.

"Wait!" Harri looked around the suite. "Where's the dog?"

"I put Dougal in our bathroom with water, kibble, and a dry towel to lay on," Steve said. "And I took him out for his constitutional this morning before you got up."

"Constitutional?" Harri rolled her eyes. "Never mind. Let's go."

As one, they all headed for the elevator. Mitzi grabbed her purse and scurried after them.

"B-b-but I can't leave the clothes here without being paid!"

Harri dug in her purse and pulled out a black credit card with the Winters Department Store logo in gold.

Mitzi gasped and hopped into the elevator car after them. "They don't issue those anymore."

"I know." Harri handed the card to her. "Now, listen to me and listen very carefully. My grandmother gave that to me when I turned thirteen. If you don't return it to me when you come back at noon, I will look for you, I will find you, and I will kill you," she finished in her best action actor impersonation.

Mitzi swallowed hard and nodded.

Harri leaned closer. "And could you please bring Gil a pair of flannel pajamas like the ones he was wearing when you arrived? His need to be washed."

"I heard that, young lady," Gil snapped.

Mitzi smiled and nodded again.

"And I will definitely buy you lunch for all your trouble," Harri offered.

"That's very generous of you," Mitzi replied. "Thank you."

The elevator doors parted, and Harri charged out into the lobby, but Tim was no longer by her side. She whirled to find him still talking to the Winters personal shopper.

"Go straight back to the store. No detours." Tim held out his hand. "Let me see your phone."

"Why?" Mitzi's eyes narrowed, but she placed her phone in his palm.

"I'm going to enter a number on one of your speed dials. If you get into trouble, anyone threatens or follows you when you leave the hotel, press the number." Tim typed as he talked. "This number goes straight to an acquaintance who can come to your assistance while we're in court."

She stared at her phone for a moment before she looked at Tim. "How did you, um, where, ur, who is—"

Harri really wished it was jealousy driving her to interrupt Tim's tête-à-tête with Mitzi. "Canyon, get a move on, or I'm leaving you here!"

"See you later, Mitzi." Tim waved at her before he jogged to catch up with Harri.

They exited the hotel. Steve must have already tipped the valet because he was helping Gil into the rear seat on the driver's side. They'd discussed the matter after Gil had gone to bed. Steve would drive and drop everybody else at the courthouse before he went to the parking garage a block down from there. It meant Gil didn't have to walk so far, and it gave her a chance to review her notes one more time.

She climbed into the front passenger seat, closed the door, and snapped the seatbelt into place. Seconds later, they were zipping through downtown's full-blown rush hour traffic.

Harri flipped through her notes. Her application to appear *pro hac vice* had been filed with the court, which allowed her to appear for a one time case in a jurisdiction in which she didn't practice. Her nerves jangled even though she'd been in federal court back in Canyon Pointe too many times to count. She didn't know this judge, didn't know what to expect from her, especially in terms of bail. Gil said the judge was a straight-shooter. However, Ultramegaperson was depending on Harri to get them out of Alcatraz, and she couldn't let them down.

Steve pulled to a stop in front of the federal court building. Gil made some comment to the kid Harri didn't catch with the roar of a bus rolling by them. Steve helped Gil to the sidewalk where Tim took over as the elderly attorney's support.

Damn, it was the damaged supporting the aged. Harri bit her tongue to keep from saying anything. Despite her regular early morning workout routine with Tim back home, she knew she couldn't do more than provide extra padding if one of them went down.

Steve honked, and the SUV pulled away from the curb. Harri waved and followed the other two men into the courthouse.

She relaxed a bit after they passed through security. No doubt Tim was armed, but whatever he had on him made it through the scanner and metal detector with no problems.

Her heart fell when she entered the courtroom. Ultramegaperson already sat at the defendant's table, well away from the other accused federal prisoners. Their rainbow ombre hair was pulled into a messy ponytail. Every bit of makeup had been scrubbed from their medium brown skin. The orange jumpsuit was two sizes too small. Even worse, the guards hadn't even let them keep their mask, which was damn illegal since they'd been charged under their hero moniker. But Ultramega-person sat before the bench with their chin held high.

Harri wanted to kill whoever had done this to Ultra. She strode down the aisle. Two men sat at the prosecutor's table, one older than her and one younger. They both glanced at her as she pushed the little swinging door of the bar open.

One of the guards moved to stop her, but she held up her visiting attorney badge that hung from her neck. The guard backed off, and she slid into the chair next to the superhero and laid her left hand over Ultra's right.

"How are you doing?" Harri murmured.

Ultra grunted. "Other than getting moved to the old solitary confinement section, I'm just peachy, darling."

"Solitary? Why?" Harri's cheeks grew hot from the outrage boiling inside her.

Ultra rolled their eyes. "Because the other idiot prisoners kept trying to beat me up and hurting themselves."

Both Tim and Gil snickered as they settled themselves on the other side of the superhero. Harri couldn't help smiling at Ultra's comment either.

The U.S. marshal who acted as bailiff entered the courtroom from the door to the judge's chambers. "All rise. The United States District Court, Northern District of California, San Francisco, is now in session. The Honorable Judge Annalise Baker presiding."

Everyone stood. Once again, Harri had to bite her tongue to keep from making a sarcastic remark as the shackles on Ultra's wrists and ankles jangled. She didn't know why the guards bothered. Ultramegaperson could shatter the steel with a good sneeze.

Judge Baker strode into the court. Her dark hair was pulled away from her face with a large mother of pearl barrette, and she wore sensible low black heels. Those were her only feminine affectations. She didn't wear the lace collar so many female judges wore as a tribute to Justice Ginsberg. To top it off, Judge Baker had one of those faces where she could be anywhere between thirty and fifty-five.

Strict, but didn't feel the need to prove herself. Harri relaxed a tiny bit more. This was the kind of judge she liked. Present the facts, no show-boating, and Ultra would be out on bail in a couple of hours.

Hopefully. Harri crossed her fingers.

Judge Baker took her chair. "Good morning, everyone. Please be seated. First arraignment to be heard is United States versus Ultramegaperson."

The younger man at the prosecutor's table stood and announced, "Assistant United States Attorneys Derek Jamison and Phillip Richards for the prosecution."

Harri and Gil stood as well. "Harriet Winters and Gilbert Wilcrest for the defense, Your Honor," she said. Court was the only time she ever said her much-resented given name aloud. As much as she loved Grandma Harri, Dad only bestowed the name on her to suck up to his mother.

"So you've turned pro-super, Ms. Winters? That's not your reputation around the country," the judge said.

"I was never anti-super, Your Honor." Harri stiffened at the rebuke. "I merely believe everyone should take responsibility for their actions when such actions damage public property."

"Mr. Wilcrest, do you agree to co-presentation of Ultramegaperson with Ms. Winters?" the judge asked.

"Yes, ma'am," Gil said.

"Ultramegaperson, do you agree to Ms. Winters and Mr. Wilcrest's representation of you in this matter?" Judge Baker continued.

"Yes, Your Honor," Ultramegaperson said.

"Then let's get the preliminaries out of the way." The judge slid on a pair of black-framed reading glasses to examine the papers in front of her. "Harriet Winters' application to appear *pro hac vice* as the defendant's counsel of record is granted." She scribbled on the proposed order.

"A point of order, Your Honor," Harri said. "My client was charged under their superhero moniker. Therefore, their mask or a reasonable substitution should have been given to them prior to any public hearing under the Superhero Act."

Judge Baker frowned as she looked at Ultra, then turned to glare at the guards. "Where's Ultramegaperson's mask?"

"Uh, I don't know," one of them answered.

"Then get them one," the judge snapped. She turned to the gallery. "If any of the journalists in the back are stupid enough to publish Ultramegaperson's unmasked likeness, I have no doubt you will be facing a civil lawsuit as well as the criminal penalties. Understood?"

A murmur of affirmatives came from the rear of the courtroom. The guard returned with a substitute mask. Gil took it from him and checked it before the elderly attorney helped Ultra put it on.

Judge Baker looked at Harri. "Do these conditions now satisfy your point of order, Ms. Winters?"

"Yes, ma'am." Harri inclined her head. "Thank you."

"All right, Ultramegaperson, here are the charges filed against you." Judge Baker's list was the same one Gil had e-mailed to Harri yesterday morning, except that the second degree murder counts now numbered

417 based on the current bodies recovered. Ultra trembled at the mention of the carnage.

Despite Ultra's diva attitude at times, they never had a casualty, much less a death, in their twenty years as a superhero. Harri and Aisha would never had taken them on if they did.

The judge took a deep breath when she finished the recitation. "Ultramegaperson, do you understand the charges levied against you?"

"Yes, ma'am, I do." The superhero's voice quavered a bit.

"Your Honor?" Harri said. At Judge Baker's nod, Harri continued. "Our client moves to dispense with the second arraignment hearing and would like to enter their plea and set bail now."

Judge Baker looked at the superhero. "Ultramegaperson, has your attorney explained what dispensing with the second arraignment hearing means? It gives your counsel less time to explore your legal options."

"Yes, ma'am, she has," they said. "I plead not guilty."

"Plea is so entered into the record." The judge's attention turned to the U.S. attorneys. "Mr. Jamison, it says here that your office has requested no bail. Want to tell me why?"

A low murmur ran through the courtroom. The prosecutor cleared his throat and adjusted his tie. Interesting. Now, what exactly was making Mr. Jamison nervous?

"We request no bail because Ultramegaperson is literally a flight risk," he said.

The entire room tittered at his statement. Even the bailiff and the court reporter smirked. Only Judge Baker and the two U.S. attorneys kept straight faces.

"Any other reason?" the judge asked dryly.

"It sets a bad precedence to allow a mass murder—" Jamison continued.

"Objection!" Harri yelled.

"This isn't a trial, counselor," Judge Baker chided before she shot Jamison a perturbed look. "However, prosecution is reminded *every-one*—" She enunciated every syllable of the word. "—is innocent until proven guilty. Anything else?"

"No, ma'am." From the red of his ears, Jamison looked like he was about to spontaneously combust.

"Ms. Winters," Judge Baker prompted.

"Ultramegaperson has never caused any casualty in their two-decade career," Harri said. "The prosecution's evidence is circumstantial. Just because my client was the only known super in the vicinity with the ability to do so doesn't mean they were the one who launched the vault into the bridge. Furthermore, Doctor Liquidation contacted my legal partner Aisha Franklin yesterday. She claims neither she or Ultramegaperson were responsible for the incident. Ms. Franklin is working on convincing Doctor Liquidation to turn herself in."

Another murmur ran through the courthouse. One that made Harri nervous.

Judge Baker gave a sad shake of her head. "You haven't seen the news this morning, have you, Ms. Winters?"

"No, ma'am." Harri cocked her head, unsure of what was happening though her instinct said it was bad. Had something gone wrong when Aisha approached Doctor Liquidation as the Ghost Owl?

"Doctor Liquidation is dead," Jamison snapped. "It was the top headline today."

Harri couldn't breathe. She would have been less surprised if the prosecutor had actually punched her in the gut.

Gil pushed himself upright. "Doctor Liquidation's death is irrelevant. Ultramegaperson has a distinguished career. If they wanted to run away, or fly away as our esteemed colleague for the prosecution pointed out, Ultramegaperson could have done so already. It is only their respect for law enforcement and this court that Ultramegaperson has remained in shackles and in custody. Quite frankly, they could have snapped the steel bonds holding them and flown out of here at any moment of this proceeding. With all due respect to the U.S. Marshals Service, there wouldn't be a damn thing anyone here could do about it."

"There's one person who could do something about it." The feminine voice rang from the back.

Harri whirled around, and gasps rose from the people in the gallery. A superhero stalked down the aisle. She wore a rich purple body suit with matching boots and mask. Her flowing shiny cape was a few shades lighter than the rest of her costume.

She stopped before the bar gate. "Violet Daze, Your Honor. I ask permission to make a statement as a friend of the court."

CHAPTER 24

The next morning, Aisha stared at the mocha Patty set in front of her on her office desk. The huge mound of whip cream couldn't disguise the rich, sweet peppermint scent, which meant Patty hadn't used the sugar-free syrup either.

"It looked like you could use the full-fat, full-sugar version this morning," Patty said.

"Thanks." Aisha knew Patty was trying to help, so why did she feel so damn guilty about the treat on her desk?

Because two women died horribly in the wee hours of this morning, and you didn't stop it, her inner voice chided.

Patty pivoted, but instead of leaving, she closed Aisha's office door and returned to sit in one of Aisha's visitor chairs. "You didn't kill Doctor Liquidation or Natalie."

"Arthur told you about last night?"

"He's worried about you." Patty leaned her elbows on the scarred surface of Aisha's secondhand desk. "And so am I. If anything, you seem more upset than when we thought Rey might be dead."

"Because there wasn't a body with him," Aisha said. "Last night, there were two dead people lying on the ground at my feet. All these abilities Xquic gifted me with, and I couldn't help anyone."

"You tried," Patti insisted. "That's more than the average person will do. They don't want to get involved, so the bullies and the jerks get away with the crap they inflict. Because no one but the real heroes try to do the right thing."

Aisha closed her eyes and exhaled. It was the same damn lecture Rey had given her when she fell into bed a few hours ago and started crying. Watching a relative die of old age was one thing. Watching a murder was a whole different, and uglier, experience.

She opened her eyes. "Patty, I know you're trying to make me feel better, but it would take a lot more mochas than you could make in a lifetime. I don't like feeling helpless, and it seems like that's how I've felt for a good chunk of my life."

"All right. I'll stop." Patty stood. "For now. Yell if you need any-thing."

"Wait." Maybe Aisha's suggestion to Qiang would help Patty, too.

Patty pivoted. "Yeah?" There was too much of a spark in her eye, so this was definitely a good idea.

"Qiang's having trouble adjusting to an empty house." Aisha smiled. "Would you like to join us for a girl's night?"

"Hell, yeah!" Patty jiggled on her toes, and her blond curls bounced. "Have you asked Susan?"

"Not yet—"

"I'll let her know!" Patty practically skipped out of the office.

Aisha chuckled and shook her head at their assistant's good cheer. She may have screwed up last night, but she could cheer up her friends tonight. The whipped cream on the mug was piled pretty high. Maybe she should grab a spoon from the break room.

She pushed her chair back, only for Patty to buzz her. "Aisha, we have a problem."

"What's wrong?"

"The blonde who dropped you off last night is at our front door."

Aisha flew to her office door, but she forced her stilettos back to the carpet. She opened the door and strode to Patty's desk. "Where is she?"

Patty pointed at the main doors.

Sure enough Harper, Doctor Liquidation's minion, or rather former minion, stared back at her.

"You want me to get Rey down here," Patty whispered.

"No, I'll take care of it." Aisha concentrated hard to keep her shoes on the art deco tiles in the reception area. It hadn't been this hard to stay on the ground since her first trimester. She pushed open the first set of bullet-proof glass doors, then the second set. The summer mid-morning air in Canyon Pointe felt like stepping into an oven.

"What are you doing here?" she demanded.

Harper lifted her chin. "I want to cut a deal."

"With?"

"The Ghost Owl." Harper's composure dissolved. "I know you don't care, b-but the doc was the closest thing I had to a mother. I want to see the people responsible for her death pay. I need the Ghost Owl's help to find them."

Aisha crossed her arms. "You blew any deal I could make for you when you and your buddies took off with the transmitters."

Harper fished around in her shoulder bag. She pulled out what appeared to be a small hot pink cosmetics case and handed it to Aisha.

She unzipped the bag. Roughly a dozen tiny electronic devices were inside. She looked up at Harper. "Are these all of the transmitters you stole?"

"Yes."

Aisha zipped the bag and slapped it against her left palm a couple of times before she made her decision. With her gesture, Patty unlocked the first set of doors. Once Aisha and Harper were in the little vestibule, humming started. Harper jumped and looked around.

"What are you doing?" she demanded.

"Scanning for weapons or listening devices."

Harper held up her hands. "I swear, no guns or plasma rifles."

"Honey, one of my very normal legal partners took out a super with a vase of roses when the idiot snuck into our building to kill her," Aisha said. Her statement was worth the shocked look on Harper's face. "I don't trust anybody, but her."

Patty buzzed the second set of doors opened. Aisha led the minion inside.

"Patty, wake up your boyfriend," Aisha ordered. "I know I said he could have the day off, but I'll make it up to him."

Their assistant mutely nodded.

"And tell Susan to get her ass in here," Aisha added. It was petty of her not to offer coffee to Harper, but Aisha wasn't about to leave the minion alone anywhere in the building, much less offer a refreshment.

She marched into her office and gestured for Harper to take one of the visitor chairs. Aisha sat in her own office chair and stared at Harper while they waited. In turn, Harper started to fidget. A few seconds later, the office door opened, and Susan poked her head inside.

"Patty said you needed me."

"Susan, this is Harper, one of Doctor Liquidation's minions."

Their newest law partner exhaled loudly, entered Aisha's office, and pinched the bridge of her nose. "One of the conditions I took this job is you and Harri both promised we wouldn't be representing any supervillians."

"She's a minion, not a supervillain," Aisha said while continuing to stare at Harper across her desk. "And she says she's willing to cut a deal."

Susan released the bridge of her nose and approached Aisha's desk. "For what?"

Aisha tossed her the cosmetics bag. Susan unzipped it and examined the contents.

She looked up at Aisha. "Are these supposed to be the stolen ink pack transmitters?"

"That's what Harper here claims."

Susan frowned. "Where are your two surviving cohorts?"

Harper stared down and licked her lips. "I gave them the keys to the doc's car and every cent I had and told them to run. Get the hell out of the country if they could. I had them leave me at the Denny's off of the North Lakeside Freeway since it was open all night. I waited there six hours, then I started walking to your office."

"Why did you tell them to run?" Aisha asked.

"A light on one of the devices came on during the drive to Canyon Pointe." Harper looked up and shrugged. "It had to be the guys that employed the doc and cut a side deal with Natalie as insurance. It didn't matter where we went. They would find us if we hung on to those things. If we dropped them somewhere, they would get the transmitters. If we destroyed them, they'd get away with Natalie's, and by extension the doc's, murders."

Aisha couldn't fault the girl's logic. "You know this means I need to call the FBI. This mess is still technically a bank robbery. Even the Ghost Owl will tell you the best you can hope for is life in prison thanks to the deaths on the Golden Gate Bridge making this an aggravated robbery, even if you weren't the ones who threw the vault at the bridge."

Harper nodded morosely.

"All right then." Aisha glanced at Susan, who shrugged to indicate she'd go along with whatever Aisha decided. "I'll call a friend at the Bureau to make the official arrest. I've got another friend who specializes in criminal defense of supervillains and minions. Is it all right if I call him and get him over here first?"

Again, Harper nodded. A tear trickled down her pale face.

"Look at it this way, Harper," Susan murmured. "With good behavior and not having any abilities, you could get parole in ten to twenty years."

The girl gulped loudly. "I-I didn't want anyone to die. That's the reason I stayed with Doctor Liquidation. She didn't kill people. No one should have died on this job."

"We know," Aisha said. "Let's just deal with one step at a time."

The intercom buzzed. Patty wouldn't interrupt a meeting unless it was an emergency.

Aisha jabbed the appropriate button on her phone set. "Yes?"

"There's an NSB Agent Wilbur Nesmith at the door asking to see you."

CHAPTER 25

At Violet Daze's appearance, Harri turned to look at Gil. He seemed as surprised as she was. She pivoted and looked at the two prosecutors. Again, they both had shocked looks on their faces.

"From the startled expressions on all the lawyers' faces, I'm assuming none of them knew about your appearance today," Judge Baker said.

"No, ma'am, they did not," Violet Daze admitted.

"Counselors, Violet Daze, side bar." The judge did not look happy.

Harry, Gil, and the two prosecutors approached the bench along with Violet Daze.

"You'd better have a damn good reason for interrupting my court," Judge Baker said in a low tone.

"I do, Your Honor." From the set of Violet Daze's mouth, she was as unhappy as the judge. "In the rush to pin the Golden Gate Bridge incident on somebody, law enforcement arrested the wrong person."

"There's a little thing called proof," Jamison snapped.

"There's video surveillance from an ATM down the street—"

"We have procedures for introducing evidence, Violet Daze," the judge admonished.

"And all of us from the superheroes to law enforcement to the attorneys are being set up to look like fools," the San Francisco super spat. "I know where the evidence is. Somebody needs to look at it."

Judge Baker rested her right index fingers on her lips as she considered the superhero's request. Finally, she said, "Ms. Winters, Mr. Wilcrest, do you have any objection to adjourning this arraignment and reconvening later this afternoon to give prosecution a chance to review this evidence?"

Harri and Gil looked at each other a moment before Harri turned back to the judge. "Actually, Your Honor, we would appreciate bail being set now. If the U.S. Attorneys Office wishes to drop charges after viewing this new evidence, our client would be even happier. In fact, I'd like to see this video Violet Daze mentioned myself."

Judge Baker looked at the prosecutors. "Mr. Jamison and Mr. Richards?"

The two men looked at each other before Jamison said, "We only reiterate our objection that Ultramegaperson is a flight risk."

"Your Honor, my client will most certainly stay in San Francisco," Harri said. "In fact, they'd like to help track down the person who killed the governor and everyone else on the Golden Gate Bridge."

"All right." Judge Baker nodded. "Let us resume this arraignment."

The attorneys returned to their benches. Violet Daze paused by Harri and rested her gloved palm on the table. "We need to talk," she whispered. "Your hotel as soon as you're done here."

When the superhero walked away, Harri's department store black card rested on the dark wood.

CHAPTER 26

Aisha wanted to bang her head against the drywall, but with her luck this week, she'd hit a support beam and bring the entire building down on everyone's heads. Dammit. She hadn't even had a chance to drink her peppermint mocha. The mound of real whipped cream was slowly melting into the hot coffee and milk.

"What do you want me to do?" Patty's voice trembled.

"Tell him I'll be right there," Aisha answered.

"Shit," Susan muttered. "How do you want to handle this?"

"No offense, but I need to be the one to talk to Eddie," Aisha said. "Take Harper to the break room. As soon as I have Agent Nesmith in my office, take her to yours, and buzz Arthur. I want him to look at those transmitters before we turn them over to the FBI or the NSB."

Susan nodded sharply and gestured for Harper to follow her. "Come on, kid."

Harper stood, but she had a worried expression on her face.

"I promise Susan won't smash an expensive lead crystal vase over your head," Aisha said.

Susan burst out laughing. "The worst thing I'll do to you is get you hyped up on my dark chocolate stash."

Aisha pushed to her feet. "Get moving, you two."

Thank goodness the breakroom was right next to her office. Susan could slip Harper in there without anyone seeing them from the front doors.

Once they were safely ensconced in the breakroom, Aisha headed for the main doors. NSB Agent Smith stood on the sidewalk. Alone.

Now that was weird. NSB agents normally worked in pairs.

Aisha shoved the exterior glass door open, and even hotter air than a half hour ago blasted her face. "Agent Nesmith?" She stuck out her right palm. "A pleasure to meet you."

He shook her hand. "Is now a bad time to talk?"

"Of course not." She forced the pleasant, bland smile she used for news conferences and reporters. "I'm sorry for the delay. I had to finish a conversation with a potential client. Please come in."

He matched her pace into the reception area, and he seemed to take in everything, including the three-story vaulted ceiling. "You folks did a nice job of restoring this building."

"You been in here before?" she asked.

"Oh, back in the day." He smiled. "My dad worked in here when Canyon Industries rented the upper floors for spillover work space."

"Patty, would you please get Agent Nesmith some coffee?"

"No, thank you." He chuckled. "It's too hot for coffee."

Patty gave him one of her perky smiles. "We have soda, diet soda, orange juice, apple juice, and bottled water."

"The water would be just fine." Nesmith smiled back.

"My office is this way." Aisha gestured to her right. Once both she and the NSB agent were inside her office, she closed the door. Again, he seemed to drink the artwork around him as he examined the prints hanging on her office walls.

He turned to Aisha. "Sara Golish?"

"How did you know?"

Nesmith chuckled. "The wife dragged me to an art show with some of her work during our vacation in New York."

"Have a seat." Aisha waved at the visitor chairs. "I'm assuming this is about my encounter with Doctor Liquidation last night."

"Yes." He moved the left chair so he could see all the windows and the door and settled into the seat. However, he remained silent.

Aisha recognized the game. She folded her hands on the top of her desk and waited with a pleasant expression glued on her face. Maybe she really was a snake in the grass like her old law school nickname implied.

Patty came in with the bottle of water and handed it to Agent Nesmith. "Do you need anything else?"

"No thanks." Aisha smiled at their assistant.

Patty bounced back out and closed the door behind her.

"You really should have reported the kidnapping, Ms. Franklin," Nesmith finally said. "It makes you look guilty as hell in Doctor Liquidation's death. Especially since her minions threatened you and your baby."

"I talked her into letting both of us go in return for setting up a meeting with the Ghost Owl." Aisha shrugged. "They even had baby supplies when they brought us to their hideout, so no harm, no foul."

"Let's cut the bullshit." He opened the water bottle and took a swig. "I'm NSB. I already looked up both you and your alter ego. You handed me the chest cam footage. I want to know what happened with the original kidnapping."

Aisha sighed before she took a sip of her mocha. Of course, he knew. She registered, tried to go legit, which meant taking the chance of whoever infiltrated the NSB and set up Rey would know about her.

By the same token, Nesmith, if he wasn't the mole, had a duty to do a thorough investigation.

"First, answer a couple of my questions," she said. "Where's your partner?"

"In the car." Nesmith snorted. "Probably with the A/C turned up as high as it'll go and some British boy band blaring through the speakers." He took another drink of water. "I thought you would be less intimidated if it were just me."

"Do you really think I intimidate easily?"

"No, ma'am, I don't." He screwed the cap back on the bottle, pulled out a pad and pen, and waited.

"Who set up my husband to be abducted by Professor Paranoia last year?" She let go of all pretense at civility.

"I don't know," Nesmith said.

She snorted.

"After Reyes Garcia was debriefed by the FBI and the NSB upon his return to the United States, there was an internal investigation." He shrugged. "Whoever sent that message to him covered their tracks well. The investigators found no evidence that the message was sent through the NBS system."

"So they believe Rey?" She found that surprising.

"Yes. The going theory with both the Feebs and NSB Internal Affairs is that whoever did it was mind-controlled by Professor Paranoia, and he or she may not even be aware of their actions."

If Nesmith wasn't lying, that meant one or more of the investigators was involved in the conspiracy. If he was feeding her a line of bullshit . . .

She needed to have a talk with Arthur about whether he could monitor the special messages in the NSB communication system that were hidden even from the system administrator.

"Any other questions?"

"Not at this time." Aisha ran through the events from dinner to Harper returning her and Mitch to the Lechuza Building.

Nesmith grunted when she finished her recitation. "Is Black Falcon willing to corroborate his parts of your story?"

"Yes," she said.

"Does Sparx know her attorney and the Ghost Owl are the same person?"

"Yes."

He frowned and looked up from his notepad. "Isn't that a conflict of interest?"

"We have structures in place. Susan Kennedy represents my interests as the Ghost Owl."

"But she's your employee?"

Aisha resisted the urge to smile. Now, he was simply testing her. "She's a full partner now. We only make bank on licensing when *all* our clients do."

"How does the Ghost Owl feel about you using his name?"

"Jatz'om Kuh, the original Ghost Owl is dead."

Nesmith grinned. "So's Captain Justice."

Aisha leaned her elbows on the table. "It's been a year since he died. Why is everyone so suddenly concerned about the original Ghost Owl? First, the U.S. attorney general demanded his whereabouts from my partner Harri Winters. Then Doctor Liquidation questioned me. Last night, two men broke into Harri's hotel room in San Francisco demanding the original. Now, you."

"Did any of you perjure yourselves when you claimed the original Ghost Owl died?"

"No," she growled.

"Then if this Mayan goddess took him to Mayan heaven, you've got nothing to worry about, right?"

"That doesn't mean someone at the NSB won't out Captain Justice and Black Falcon as the same person." She deliberately narrowed her eyes. "I would be very unhappy if that happened."

Nesmith scowled back. "Are you threatening me, Ms. Franklin?"

She shot him a vicious smile. "I can do more damage to the NSB legally than I can with superstrength."

"And that would be a good way to lose custody of your son," he said.

"Corvus already tried." She leaned back in her chair. "Look what happened to them."

He nodded sharply. "Point taken."

"I'm glad we understand each other."

Nesmith put his notebook and pen back in his suit jacket pocket. They both stood at the same time.

"One more thing, Ms. Franklin." He was back to the folksy charm of last night. "I need to take those transmitters from the Federal Reserve back with me." He made a self-deprecating gesture. "You understand, of course."

"On one condition," she said.

"You have possession of stolen property. You don't really have a legal leg to stand on here."

"Not that." She rounded her desk. "I want someone from the FBI to witness the change in possession." She smiled. "You understand, of course."

Nesmith smiled back. "In this case, I certainly do."

CHAPTER 27

Harri swallowed hard and slipped the black plastic into the business card slot of her folder. A disguised superhero had managed to enter their suite, and they'd all been too preoccupied to notice. Not even Tim. Damn, she was good.

"If you'd like to finish your statement, Ms. Winters," Judge Baker prompted.

Harri struggled to collect her thoughts. "As I said a few moments ago, Ultramegaperson has never had a casualty in their twenty years of battling evil. We ask they be released on their own recognizance."

"Given the circumstances and both parties' requests, I hereby set bail at twenty-thousand for Ultramegaperson." Judge Baker shot annoyed looks at the attorneys at both tables. "And no more grandstanding by either side, or I'll hold you in contempt. That goes for you, too, Violet Daze."

Everyone scolded answered with variations of "Yes, ma'am" or "Yes, Your Honor".

"What's next?" Ultramegaperson whispered.

"We'll take care of the bail and collect you when you're released." Harri tried to give them a reassuring smile. "We already have a suite a few blocks from here and we'll strategize after we get some lunch."

As the guards guided Ultramegaperson away, Harri and her team collected their things so the next defense team could work. She looked around but Violet Daze had already slipped out of the court room.

"What's wrong?" Tim whispered.

"I'll tell you in the SUV."

Steve intercepted them on their way out of the doors of the courtroom, and he took Gil's arm. "Can superheroes just approach the bench like that?"

"Not normally," Harri said. "But this is anything but a normal situation."

Gil snorted. "That's for sure."

Once bail had been made for Ultra and they were released, Steve retrieved their rental vehicle. It was a tight squeeze with an extra person in the back seat. Thank goodness, they only had a short ride.

When Steve pulled into traffic, Harri announced, "We're going to have a guest in our suite when we get back." She held up her Winters black card.

"Good," Tim said. "That means Mitzi's safe."

Harri twisted to look at him in the back seat. "Excuse me?"

"I gave Mitzi Violet Daze's number," he said.

"I see." Harri wanted to scream. How many super-exes did her boyfriend have? "I guess I should be glad this one was a superhero."

"What's going on?" Ultramegaperson said. They were back into their glittery superhero outfit even though it had serious jail stink.

"Mom and Dad are about to have a fight over some ex-girlfriends of his," Steve said.

"Oooo!" Ultramegaperson chuckled. "Do dish, Stephen."

"My love life is not a topic for discussion," Tim snapped.

Ultramegaperson ignored him. "So which delectable supervil-lainesses caught Timmy's attention? Jeremy swore he was practically a monk."

"Miss Purrception and Doctor Liquidation," Steve said.

"Would you two drop it?" Tim groaned.

"Oh! I love it!" Ultramegaperson clapped their hands and giggled. "Timmy has a taste for bad girls."

"Your head of security is making time with known felons?" Gil looked appalled.

"Was!" Tim yelled. "Past tense, and it was before you were in kin-dergarten, Steve, so shut it. Harri, Violet Daze and I were never a thing. The same for Doctor Liquidation! And I don't appreciate our personal business being discussed in front of a client!"

"Fellow counsel doesn't want to hear it either," Gil grumbled.

Ultramegaperson leaned forward and not-so-subtly said, "Stephen, you and I need to get a drink later."

"I wouldn't be hitting on my intern, Ultra," Harri warned.

"Why? Jealous much, honey?"

"Not me. Sparx." Harri looked over her shoulder and grinned at the superhero. "She'll fry your ass if you mess with her boyfriend."

"Sparx?" Ultra placed their hand on their chest in mock horror. "I didn't think the grumpy gus had it in her. Go cougar power!"

"May we please focus on our case?" Gil pleaded. "Did Violet Daze say what other evidence she had regarding Ultramegaperson?"

"No," Harri said. "Just that she'd meet us at the hotel because she needed to speak to us in private."

Even Ultra remained silent the rest of the way to the hotel.

⁕

At the hotel's elevator, Tim stopped everyone from entering the car. "Ultramegaperson and I will go up first. Harri, I'll text you once we've cleared the suite."

"And make sure you and Violet Daze are on the same page in front of your current girlfriend?" Ultra said with a teasing tone.

Tim ignored them and pressed the button for the suite.

"Do you always have this much drama with your staff, Harri?" Gil asked.

"Nah." She smiled at him. "It's usually much, much worse."

Gil checked the hallway around them. "This looks like an excellent spot for an ambush."

"Normally, I'd agree," Harri said mildly. The last thing she'd do is out Steve.

The elderly attorney stuck his hand in his suit jacket pocket and fidgeted. Now, why was he acting so nervous? The arraignment went better than she thought it would.

Her phone vibrated in her pocket. She pulled it out to check the message. "All clear." She reached over and punched the elevator button.

Inside the car, she slid her keycard into the slot. Maybe Gil was right to be nervous. The NSB still wasn't sure how many supers besides Black Death were part of Corvus's scheme. What if Violet Daze was one of them?

Harri shut down that train of thought. She was beginning to sound like Tim. However, the men who broke into their first hotel room last night were equally obsessed except they were looking for the original Ghost Owl.

She frowned. Their attackers had hit hers and Tim's room first. She'd assumed she was the main target, but what if they knew Tim was asleep and was therefore an easier target?

The elevator doors opened, and she marched to the main door. Once again, she shoved her card key in the slot. Steve inserted himself between her and the lever and entered first. He pulled the door open wider.

Tim and Violet Daze stood on each side of a man tied to a chair. Their prisoner's eyes were a weird purple color. Violet Daze was actively using her power to keep him under control. Ultramegaperson sat on the farthest couch with a frown on their face. Dougal stood on the arm of the closest couch and growled.

"What the hell?" Harri stared at the scene.

"Mr. Canyon was right." Violet Daze smiled. "Someone did decide your personal shopper could be used as leverage against you." She reached up and pulled back her cowl, revealing a familiar face.

"Mitzi?" Harri stared. She'd been hoping she was wrong.

"No." Violet Daze shook her head. "I know the real Mitzi Brennan. She's normally very professional, but she heard about you in the news. When she was assigned as your personal shopper, she got scared and called me."

She turned to Tim. "What I want to know is where you got that number? I've only given it to three people. One of them is supposed to be dead, and I know you aren't the other two."

"I want to know how you managed to get into our suite," Tim growled.

Violet Daze held up a hotel key card. "The asshole who tried to abduct me had this on him."

"That still doesn't answer—" Tim started.

"Can we deal with this jerk in the chair first?" Harri placed her cross body bag and her file on a nearby table and turned to Violet Daze.

"Then I'll make him tell you how he got your number." She glared at Tim. "Privately."

"All right," Violet Daze said. "If Ultramegaperson trusts you, I'm willing to go on a little faith."

"No!"

Everyone whirled around to find Gil with some kind of weird weapon in his hand.

"Let your prisoner go," he demanded.

"Gil, what the hell—" Harri started.

"Shut up, Winters, or I shoot your boy toy!" He waved his weapon. "All you supers get over by the sliding glass doors. And if you think my little friend won't hurt you, think again."

Ultramegaperson and Violet Daze moved toward the exit to their suite's balcony.

"You, too, fake intern," Gil ordered.

"I'm not a fake intern," Steve protested indignantly.

Gil pressed a button on his weapon. Green plasma hit Steve square in the chest. The kid flew backward and crashed into the kitchenette's full-sized refrigerator.

"Steve!" Harri ignored the crazy attorney and ran to the kid's side. An ugly third-degree burn covered a good eight-inch circle in the middle of his chest. Harri's breath seized in her own lungs. That weapon would have disintegrated her or Tim.

However, if she could keep Gil distracted, Ultra or Violet could get that weapon out of his hands.

She slowly rose to her feet. "You're the one who let those goons know Tim was asleep in our first hotel room. You set your own damn house on fire. You let the goons know about the personal shopper. And you were pretending to limp so you'd fall behind and slip this guy your key card." She shook her head. "What I don't get is why, Gil?"

"Because I'm tired of your holier-than-thou attitude," he responded. "You're just like your grandmother. Tearing down everything I worked for!"

"The laws you drafted don't protect the citizens from the supers," Harri argued. "In fact, it sets up assholes like Seismic Shift to abuse the system."

"No, it was designed to protect the supers from themselves!" Gil stomped his foot. His face was nearly purple with his fury. "With government oversight, everyone would be safe! But no-o-o," he drawled sarcastically. "They need their civil liberties! They're not people! They're weapons. And this idiot couldn't do his damn job!"

He shot the goon in the chair. The poor man's head disappeared in a blaze of green plasma. Harri's stomach rebelled at the sight. Dougal started barking hysterically.

"Shut up, Dougal!" Gil roared. When the dog quieted, he shook his head sadly. "All we wanted was the location of the first Ghost Owl, but—"

Harri could practically see the wheels turning inside his head.

Gil smiled. "Clever girl. Hide the original right under everyone's nose." He glanced at the still form of Steve. "The kid's too young. The Ghost Owl's been around for a couple of decades." He pointed his weapon at Tim. "By default—"

"No!" Harri stepped between Gil's weapon and Tim. "He's not a super, Gil."

"Because he figured out how to transfer his powers to the new Ghost Owl," Gil accused.

"I never had powers." Tim moved to Harri's side. "All I had was a flaming desire for revenge and a lot of money to burn."

"Stop, Gil." Steve grunted and winced as he tried to get to his feet. "They're lying to protect me. The original Ghost Owl was my biological father. Let them live, and I'll go with you."

"Sorry, kid, it's too, t-too . . ." In slow motion, Gil's eyes rolled to the back of his head and his body sagged to the floor.

CHAPTER 28

Aisha breathed a sigh of relief when Special Agent Eddie Lewis and his partner arrived at the Lechuza Building. He may be Harri's ex-husband, but he was the only law enforcement officer Aisha trusted in Canyon Pointe.

Especially these days.

Patty buzzed the two FBI agents into the reception area. The heels of their dress shoes clacked against the black and white tiles.

"What's the emergency?" Eddie asked as he examined the NSB agent.

"This is Agent Nesmith from the National Superhero Bureau," Aisha started the round of introductions. When she finished, she added, "One of Doctor Liquidation's minions left a present on our doorstep this morning."

"The ink pack transmitters from the San Francisco Federal Reserve heist?" Eddie asked.

"Yes," Aisha affirmed. "If you gentlemen will excuse me for a moment, I'll retrieve them from our secure storage."

She headed back to Susan's office. When she opened the door and entered, she laid her right index finger over her lips.

Susan nodded and handed over the hot pink cosmetic bag. Arthur had a worried expression on his face, or more worried than normal. Harper sat on Susan's couch and trembled.

Aisha left, closing the door behind her, and marched back to the reception area.

"I want a dated receipt once you've checked the contents," Aisha said as she handed the bag to Agent Nesmith.

"You definitely like dotting your 'i's and crossing your 't's, don't you?"

Eddie crossed his huge arms. "Actually, I'd like a copy of that receipt, too."

"I'll need to go out my car—" Nesmith started.

"Oh, you don't have to go out in the dreadful heat." Patty's perky smile had just a hint of evil. "I've already drafted the form for you, and I am a notary." She held up the sheet of paper for Nesmith to sign.

He unzipped the bag and checked the contents before he practically ripped the pen out of Patty's hand. He signed as recipient, Aisha signed as grantor, and Eddie and his partner signed as witnesses. Patty stamped the receipt, scanned it, and printed copies for everyone. Nesmith snatched his copy and stomped out of the office without another word.

Eddie shook his head. "What crawled up his ass?"

"An uppity black woman," Aisha said sourly.

Eddie's partner wasn't sure whether to laugh until Eddie himself did.

"How's Rey and Mitch?" Eddie asked. "I haven't seen either one since the baby was born."

As if in answer to his question, the antique elevator ground to a halt, and Rey with Mitch in his chest carrier and the diaper bag slung over his shoulder raced around the corner.

"Baby, I can't wait for Molly. Hey, Eddie!" Rey blurted as he divested himself of baby and paraphernalia. "Anna was showing Emilio how to fillet white fish and cut herself pretty good."

"Go, go, go," Aisha said as she cradled Mitch in her arms.

"Talk to you later." Rey pecked her on the lips and rushed out the doors. Thankfully, not at superspeed.

"Hey there, little guy." Eddie made faces at Mitch until the baby burbled and waved his tiny fists.

His partner rolled his eyes. "So it's not just your kids you do that to."

"Can I?" Eddie held out his hands.

"Sure." Aisha handed over the baby. As much as she wanted Eddie and his partner out of here, if she rushed him, Eddie would know something was up.

Thankfully, Molly arrived after five minutes of watching the huge, white FBI man playing peek-a-boo with Mitch.

"Hey, big guy!" Molly smiled at Mitch. "Did you find a new playmate?" She glanced at Aisha. "Has he had lunch yet?"

"Not yet." Aisha smiled as Eddie reluctantly handed Mitch over to Molly. "Rey had to leave for work early. You want to take Mitch up to the loft. I'll be up in a few minutes."

At Eddie's forlorn expression watching Molly walk away with the baby, Aisha laughed. "Do I need to set up a playdate with you two?"

Eddie grunted. "I think it would be a great idea for all our kids, but unfortunately, you're guilty by association." He smiled. "But I'm not going to stop trying. When she gets back from San Francisco, tell Harri . . ."

"I will." Aisha nodded. After their not-quite-bitter divorce, it was good to see both Eddie and Harri come to terms with it and start acting civil. And that was probably Sarah's real problem with the situation. Civil meant the possibility Eddie saw his ex in a new light.

Once the FBI agents departed, Aisha headed back to Susan's office.

"Well?" Susan asked when she entered.

"The NSB now has the transmitters," Aisha said.

"What about my deal?" Harper's eyes widened.

"He didn't say a damn word about you." Aisha crossed her arms and shot the former minion a pointed look.

"But they were using the transmitters to track Harper the entire time," Arthur said. "They knew she was here. Why not arrest her?"

"Because she's not a super, so they don't care," Aisha said.

Arthur rolled his eyes. "Alex, what's the definition of illogical?"

"We really need to get you on Jeopardy!" Susan exclaimed.

"Wh-what do I do now?" Harper wailed.

"Arthur, take Harper down to Celia's bodega," Aisha said. "Tell Celia she needs a really cold ice cream from deep in the freezer."

"But I'm lactose intolerant!" Harper shivered as Arthur approached her.

"Don't worry," he assured her. "It's code for getting you out of the city."

However, the former minion didn't look one bit reassured. But she did follow Arthur out of the office.

Once they were gone, Susan eyed Aisha. "She's going to need cash."

Aisha sighed. "I know."

Susan leaned over and opened the bottom drawer of her desk. After a series of clicks, she straightened and held up a bank bundle of twenty-dollar bills. "My contribution to the relocate Harper fund."

"You don't have to—" Aisha started.

"She's a good kid," Susan murmured. "She just got a little turned around is all. And I know damn well you're going to give her money, too, so shut up and take it."

Aisha accepted the bundle. "Thank you. I need to feed Mitch before I fly her to Hermanville."

After telling Patty she'd be taking a long lunch, Aisha rode the elevator to her flat. Despite everything that had happened over the last thirty-six hours, helping Harper start over was the one thing that felt right.

CHAPTER 29

Harri and Tim charged for the elderly man, but Ultramegaperson beat them to Gil.

"He's not breathing," Ultra said.

"No heartbeat," Tim added.

Together, they straightened out Gil's form. Ultra began chest compressions, and Tim performed mouth-to-mouth resuscitation. Harri ran for the hotel phone and called 9-1-1.

Dougal ran in circles around his human and whined.

"9-1-1. What is your emergency?" the operator chirped.

"We have an elderly man who collapsed, Caucasian, eighty-nine years of age," Harri barked. "He has no pulse and he's not breathing. People have started CPR, but he's non-responsive." She rattled off the name and address of their hotel. "We're in Suite A."

"Harri," Ultra called out. "I don't think we can wait. Ask the operator where the nearest hospital is."

"Forget the paramedics. I've got a superhero with flight capabilities on the scene," Harri said. "What's the closest hospital?"

Thankfully, the operator didn't argue. She gave Harri the name and address of the nearest medical center.

Harri repeated the information to Ultra as they lifted Gil in their arms. Tim jogged out to the elevator. Luckily, it was still on their floor.

"We'll meet you at the hospital," Harri yelled as the doors closed.

"I've notified the hospital's ER of the superhero's arrival," the operator said. "Do you need further assistance, ma'am?"

"Yes, can you connect me with the NSB?" Out in the foyer, Harri could hear Violet Daze and Tim talking.

The pair came back into the sitting room and started checking on Steve and his awful wound. Harri had to turn away to keep from throwing up.

"NSB, Agent Blackwood, how can I help you?"

Harri spilled out the story of Gil's betrayal, the dead minion in their suite, and Gil's collapse.

"Where is Mr. Wilcrest right now?" Blackwood asked.

"Ultramegaperson just took him to the hospital."

"And this plasma weapon?"

"It's lying on the floor." Harri gulped for air as the murder replayed in her mind. "I think one of us kicked it out of the way when we started CPR, but otherwise we haven't touched it."

"Leave it there, and don't touch anything else if you can help it," Blackwood said. "We have a team on the way."

"Thank you." Harri disconnected the call.

"My Dazemobile is downstairs in employee parking." Violet Daze grunted as she and Tim helped Steve upright. "I can get your intern to someone who can help him."

Sweat rolled down Steve's face, and his skin had taken on a sickly green color. The poor kid appeared to be going into shock. Harri looked at Tim, and he nodded.

"All right." Harri nodded, too.

Tim helped the superhero get Steve to the elevator. "You can override the car's control—"

"Don't sweat it. I've done this before." Violet Daze grinned at him. "I'm just glad you're not dead, old man."

Once the superhero and Steve left, Tim walked back into the sitting room. He and Harri stared at each other.

"What now?" he said as he pulled her into his arms.

"We wait for the NSB." She hid her face in his chest and tried not to think about the headless corpse a few feet away.

Dougal let out a mournful howl by the elevator.

All in all, Harri only had to tell two lies. One was a lie of omission. She left out any mention of Tim as the original Ghost Owl. The second one was that Steve hurt himself attempting to take on Gil, only to trip over Dougal. She was sure the kid would forgive her for that one.

Surprisingly, petting the dog helped Harri keep her composure during her NSB interview.

Steve and Violet Daze returned to the hotel before the NSB finished. Both of them stuck to the script Tim and Harri agreed on and texted to Steve.

When the NSB asked Steve about his injuries, he claimed it was a couple of bruised ribs from landing flat on his face. He then joked that it was a good thing he wasn't a super. Otherwise, he would have accidentally leveled the city.

Harri had to kick his ankle to stop him from embellishing. She was sure she'd bruised the bones in her big toe for her action.

Once the NSB finished their investigation of the suite and removed the dead minion, the hotel manager politely, but firmly, asked Harri to never stay at his hotel again.

Violet Daze changed back into her Mitzi persona. Harri paid for the clothes Gil had worn to court and added a healthy tip for the real Mitzi. Violet Daze was kind enough to help pack up their belongings.

"What do we do with the dog?" Harri asked.

"Actually, Aunt Mitzi would foster him in a heartbeat," Violet Daze said.

They all stared at her.

"Well." She shrugged. "You guys have told me all of your secrets." She held up her index finger. "Oh! The thing I wanted to say in court. There's an ATM video showing an unknown woman tossing the Federal Reserve vault in the direction of the Golden Gate Bridge. When it's cross-referenced with the Fed's security cameras, she looks to be one of Doctor Liquidation's minions, and Ultramegaperson is nowhere near the vault at the same time."

"How do you know this?" Harri asked.

"My boyfriend is a police inspector," Violet Daze said.

Despite all of the issues with Harri's team's stay, the hotel manager sent up a couple of bellhops to help them with their luggage.

Or maybe to make sure Harri's party actually left.

They parted ways with Violet Daze and Dougal in the lobby.

The guys along with the bellhops and their trolleys headed out to valet parking. Harri approached the desk, her heart tripping at the thought of the bill. The manager burst out from the employees-only entrance and shooed away the desk clerk. Harri tried not to wince.

"All I can do, besides apologize again, is pay the bill."

The manager waved his hand. "Your charges have already been covered."

"What? How?" Harri stared at him.

"The NSB took care of the damages, and Ms. Violet Daze paid for your rooms." He pulled an envelope from his inside breast pocket and held it out to Harri. "Ms. Daze did ask that I give this to you."

Harri took the envelope and nodded. "Thank you."

Now, why the hell would the NSB pay for the damages? Something definitely didn't smell right.

She opened the envelope, pulled out the note and read it.

Harri,

    Consider your hotel bill as a down payment on my retainer. I'll be in touch.

                                  Violet

P.S. I didn't sleep with your boyfriend. Like, ewwww!

Harri laughed on her way out the hotel door.

⁂

Ultramegaperson was waiting for them when Harri's team arrived at the hospital ER.

"The docs did their damnedest, Harri." They sadly shook their head. "They think it was a massive stroke near the brain stem. It would have killed him instantly no matter what we did. I'm sure you can find out more after the autopsy."

Harri nodded. "The NSB—"

"Already come and gone." Ultra smiled. "Timmy gave me the heads-up. I also heard from Violet you got kicked out of your hotel."

"We'll find another one—"

"No." Ultra waggled their index finger. "You three are coming home with me."

"But—" she started.

"No arguing!" Ultra stomped their foot, causing a hairline crack in the floor tile.

Harri was too tired to argue. "Fine."

Tim sidled up to Ultra. "You are going to have to teach me that trick."

Chapter 30

Aisha was exhausted when she entered the Owl's Nest. Flying Harper to the Hermanville bus station had been exhausting. Worse, she hadn't had two seconds to call Harri to find out how Ultramegaperson's arraignment had gone. But what Aisha really wanted was a cool bath, a glass of wine, and five minutes that didn't involve a crisis of some sort.

She peeled out her sweaty Ghost Owl outfit and left it next to the special cleaning machine. She'd deal with it tomorrow. Besides, she had a couple of spares upstairs. She had Jeremy make her extras after Mitch's diaper exploded all over her superhero outfit right before a charity event last month.

She grabbed her phone out of its pocket and padded out of the Owl's Nest and up the stairs in the tank and boy shorts she wore under her uniform. The cold metal steps felt wonderful on her bare feet.

When she reached the first floor, office doors were closed and Patty's equipment on her desk was shut down. Good. Aisha retrieved a cold bottle of water from the break room refrigerator and walked to her office, chugging the water as she went. Maybe she should have grabbed another bottle.

She flopped on the couch in her office and speed-dialed Harri's number. It rang once.

"What the hell did you do to Doctor Liquidation!"

"Hello to you, too," Aisha snapped.

"I'm sorry," Harri said. For once, she sounded like she meant it. "I got blind-sided at the arraignment this morning with the news of her death."

"I'm sorry, too." Aisha swallowed the rest for her water and tossed the bottle in the general direction of her waste basket. She'd sort the recyclables later. "I heard on the radio Gil suffered a massive stroke this afternoon."

"Oh, that's not even the beginning of the story." Harri filled Aisha in on everything that happened since the plane landed yesterday.

Good grief. Harri had only been gone for a day.

"If the hotel kicked you out, where are you right now?" Aisha asked.

"I am wrapped in a fluffy white bath robe, reclining on a lounge next to a heated pool, and drinking a margarita at Ultramegaperson's estate in Oakland."

"Bitch."

In the background, Aisha heard someone yell something.

"In case you did not hear that, Ultra says to get your ass on a plane and come out tonight."

"I'm too tired." Aisha related her own thirty-six-hour adventure.

"Am I too drunk and you too tired to figure out the connection here?" Harri said before she slurped.

"Probably—wait!" Aisha sat up on the couch. "Did you say one of Liquidation's minions was filmed throwing the vault?"

"Yep." Harri slurped again.

"Dark hair, but no magenta highlights, right?"

"Yep." Harri slurped her damn margarita for a third time.

"That sounds like Liquidation's major domo Natalie," Aisha said.

"She's the one who killed Liquidation before someone assassinated her."

Harri swore a few colorful oaths. In the background, Ultramegaperson shouted, "Don't waste good tequila, bitch!"

"Shut up, queen! We just proved your innocence!" Harri yelled back.

CHAPTER 31

Harri wasn't sure if she was happy to be home or not. She'd been back in Canyon Pointe for three days, ever since the feds dropped the charges against Ultramegaperson two days after the arraignment. And she'd ignored her firm in order to prove her worst fears wrong.

Except that wasn't happening.

When the loft door rolled open, Harri looked up from her seat on the floor.

"Hey, honey, you feel like—" Tim's smile fell as he took in the stacks of paper around her. "Did one of your filing cabinets explode?"

"Come in. Close the door and lock it."

He did as she ordered. If only the clawing panic in her gut would go away as easily.

"Harri?" Tim carefully skirted the piles and perched on the arm of her turquoise couch. "What's going on?"

"I-I think Grandma Harri did something really, really bad." Her breath shuddered as she released it. "And I'm not sure what to do."

"Honey, start at the beginning. You're not making any sense."

She took another shuddering breath. "Before Grandma Harri died, she rented a storage locker in the name of Aisha's dad. The story she told Marvin was there were things she wanted to make sure I got, and she didn't trust Dad."

"Sounds reasonable considering what you've told me about all three of them." Tim leaned his elbows on his new knees and rested his chin on his fists. "I take it this stuff was in the locker?"

"Yeah, after she died, Marvin and Betty paid the locker rental until I turned twenty-one." Harri swallowed hard. Maybe she should have poured whiskey for both her and Tim before she dove into this, but she couldn't burden Aisha or Jeremy with this crap. Tim, however, understood the bullshit of rich people's ugly secrets. He'd kept the secret of his grandfather Jack and Grandma Harri's affair for decades after their deaths.

Long after Canyon Industries collapsed and Dad sold the Winters Department Store chain to an eastern conglomerate.

"On my birthday, Marvin gave me an envelope from Grandma Harri. Inside was a letter, a key, and the business card of the storage company. She said there was a locker with some important things, and that she only trusted me with them. I figured it was some family heirlooms, silver or china. Something she didn't want Dad to pawn for his drug habit."

Tim didn't ask any questions. He didn't even speak a word. He simply waited for her to get out whatever she needed to say.

"I never even opened the locker until now," Harri admitted. "At the time Marvin gave me the key, I was in my senior year of college and trying to figure out how to pay for law school. Every time I moved, I'd see the key and think I should clean out that locker. That I was wasting money paying for it. And every time it hurt too much to go to the locker and clean it out."

"What changed?" Tim asked softly. "Is it because I was feeling you out about making us official?"

"No." Harri shook her head and swiped at the single tear that escaped. It had to be all the dust from the boxes. "It was things Gil said. He claimed he met Grandma Harri at a fundraiser Eagle Forever used to hold and mentioned she was a major contributor to the Superhero Legal Defense Fund. And then his shouting right before he died, about the government controlling the supers."

"Your grandmother gave to a lot of causes." Tim shrugged. "So did my grandfather."

"And Seismic Shift murdered Eagle Forever." She threw up her hands. "Why wait until he was a wizened old man? What possible danger could a retired centenarian superhero be to Corvus?"

"Maybe Eagle Forever threatened to out Corvus?" Tim mused. "Eagle Forever was Trubble's mentor at one time. But he wouldn't have kept any evidence at the Lake County Retirement Home. Too many people around to keep whatever he had safe."

"That's what I thought, too." She grabbed the pictures she had been looking at when Tim came home. "And then I wondered if maybe Grandma Harri wasn't doing an old friend a favor." She handed the pictures to Tim.

"Who's the family?" Tim asked. "Cousins of yours?"

"I don't think so." Harri drew her knees to her chest and wrapped her arms around her bare legs. Despite the heat of the day, she was chilled to the bone. "That's Mr. and Mrs. Linwood Baxter and their daughter."

"Eagle Forever and his family?" Both of Tim's eyebrows shot towards his hairline.

Harri nodded. "From the date of the developer's mark, it wasn't too long after World War II."

Tim slipped the antique photo to the bottom of the stack and examined the second one. "Why is Eagle Forever with a different woman and baby?"

"That's his daughter Lydia and his grandson." Harri sighed. "Baxter's wife worked for the U.S. Army on the Manhattan Project during the war. She died of cancer shortly before their grandson was born. Allegedly, the daughter and grandson were both killed in a car accident a few months after that picture was taken. The next photo is dated six months later."

Tim flipped to the next picture. "What the fuck!" His jaw dropped open, and he stared at the third photo for a long time before he looked at Hatti. "This can't be right."

"Someone had to help Trubble start Corvus." Harri's vision grew blurry. "If Linwood Baxter refused, it's entirely possible Grandma Harri did."

She didn't need to see the picture Tim stared at again. The image of Grandma Harri on the left side of Lydia Baxter-Murray, Lydia's toddler son in her arms, and a very young Byron S. Trubble on Lydia's right was seared into her brain.

CHAPTER 32

Monica Reinhold, AKA Miss Purrception, smiled at the inmate next to her on the pullup bar in the exercise yard of Mauvaises Prison. Hard Knock grinned back. He was the toughest supervillain in the entire prison. They'd also come to an understanding years earlier. He'd watch her back if she got caught. In return, she'd include him in her prison escapes.

Unfortunately, being the toughest super did not equate to being the smartest. He'd get busted for something within a month of their escape. Usually for something stupid like shoplifting or an illegal amount of pot. Then the local cops didn't learn who they had on their hands until it was too late. Usually after several police vehicles were trashed and several cops ended up in the hospital. Hard Knock would end up back at Mauvaises because a conventional prison couldn't hold him, and it was too risky to transport him to Alcatraz.

Then he'd have to wait until she was sentenced before he could get out. Those stays were getting longer and longer since she was getting caught less and less.

The crowd of inmates around them quieted as the last round of betting finished. Mr. Anole stood in front of them. Unfortunately due to his peculiar ability, his skin was a constant neon yellow thanks to the prison's jumpsuits.

"Go!" Mr. Anole yelled.

Monica and Hard Knock started pullups as fast as they could. The other inmates shouted encouragement or derogatory remarks depending on who they bet on to win.

All of the sudden the crowd went silent. Not like the silence when a guard approached either. Monica looked down. A tall, dark-haired man stood below them. The entire crowd gave Black Death a very wide berth.

"Hard Knock, hold up," she said.

"So you can beat me again," he responded. "No flippin' way!"

Monica ignored him and released her hold on the pullup bar. She dropped to the ground and straightened, keeping her attention glued on super before her. "What do you want?"

"The boss wants to talk to you," Black Death said.

"I have nothing to say to him." Monica turned away.

Before she could take a step, Black Death grabbed her arm, the threat implicit in his very touch.

"Let her go." Hard Knock dropped to the ground, too.

Monica held up her free hand. "Let's hear his boss out."

"You can't trust Mr. GQ here or his boss." Hard Knock spat a loogie at Black Death's feet.

"But you trust her?" Black Death eyebrows rose.

"I like her." Hard Knock cocked his head. "I don't like you."

"Lighten up, Knock." She looked at Black Death's hand and then his face again. He released her arm.

"This way," he said.

Finally. She'd had to play hard to get for the last several months. It was the only way to lure in Black Death and his boss.

Once Monica was back in her cell, she climbed into the top bunk and retrieved the tiny, cheap flip phone from its hiding spot inside the steel frame. She texted that contact had been made.

A few seconds later, Carol Inunza texted back.

Understood. Plan in motion.

Monica hid her phone again and stared at the ceiling, hoping the attorney knew what the hell she was doing. For the first time in decades, Monica felt unsure. Because if she failed, she had no doubt Black Death and his boss, former head of Corvus, Byron S. Trubble, wouldn't settle with killing just her. They'd kill her mother and daughters out of spite, too.

Can Harri figure out the real connection between her grandmother, the murder of a retired superhero, and the former leader of Corvus? And what exactly is Miss Purrception planning with Judge Inunza's wife? Find out in the next thrilling volume of 888-555-HERO!

Turn the page for an exciting preview of *Hero In Camera*!

Hero In Camera
©2020, Suzan Harden

Harri Winters smiled across her office desk at Mother Defiant, who sat on one of Harri's visitor chairs. The superhero's white coif, veil and wimple were at odds with her skintight black unitard and shiny black boots. Everything happened exactly as Winters and Franklin's newest partner Susan Kennedy had predicted a little over a year ago.

"I don't understand why I can't simply talk to Susan," Mother Defiant said haughtily.

"Because I'm the senior partner." Harri kept the smile plastered on her face though she really wanted to leap over her desk and smack the attitude from the superhero's pretty face. "I do the intake interviews, but the entire partnership has a vote on whether to accept a new client."

"But I'm not a new client!" Mother Defiant protested.

"You are to this firm." Harri shrugged. "And frankly, we'll be taking a very serious look at you. Especially after you dumped Susan for Dewey and Cheatham."

Mother Defiant's cheeks flushed bright pink. At least, she had the grace to be embarrassed. When she could finally meet Harri's eyes again, she said, "I should have known they were only using me. The reason I want to speak with Susan is I owe her a very big apology."

At the knock on Harri's office door, she yelled, "Come in."

Tim Canyon sauntered in with Mother Defiant's cell phone in his hand. "I've cleaned off the spyware and added extra protection. No one will be tracking you anymore."

"Tracking me?" Mother Defiant looked appalled.

"Was it the source of Susan's infection last year?" Harri asked.

"Definitely." Tim held out the phone to Mother Defiant. "You're clean now, but you might want to inform any superheroes you've come in contact with over the last year. I'll clean up their devices free of charge."

"What?" Mother Defiant looked wildly at Harri and Tim, totally flabbergasted. "Who?"

"Corvus used you to get a bug into our office last year," Harri said.

"I wasn't a part of that crap!" Mother Defiant protested. "Not to mention they're all in jail now." Her eyes widened as she put two and two together. "Dewey and Cheatham were part of Corvus?"

"We don't know anything for sure at this point," Harri said as evenly as she could. While the Winters & Franklin staff suspected a link between the rival law firm and the out-of-control black ops group, the last thing Harri needed was a slander lawsuit against her fledgling business.

"If you need anything else, buzz me." Tim winked at Harri before he sauntered out of her office, closing the door behind him.

"I still can't believe your head of security is Tim Canyon."

Harri smirked at the superhero's comment. "He was acquitted during his murder trial, and the Ghost Owl exposing Corvus proved Seismic Shift killed Tim's wife and son."

Mother Defiant sagged in her chair. "Is that why I can't talk to Susan directly? She thinks I set her up? That I was part of the Corvus conspiracy?"

Damn. Harri hated even thinking about those assholes. But she knew the FBI sweep didn't capture all of Corvus's allies either. While she wanted to give Mother Defiant the benefit of the doubt, she couldn't risk the lives of everyone she loved.

"As I said, the entire partnership will discuss whether or not to take you on as a client," Harri said firmly. "My question is why do you want a firm outside of Hermanville."

Mother Defiant took a deep breath. "I've been dating Blue Racer. Once Dewy and Cheatham charged me for every little thing, I barely have enough from my licensing contracts to live on, and I'm tired of ramen noodles every night for supper. Blue said he was super happy with what your firm did for him, and when I found out my old attorney worked here, I decided to change representation."

Harri nodded. "All right. I'll start calling your references this afternoon. Assuming everyone gets back to me right away, you should hear from me in two days."

"Thank you for considering me as a client." Mother Defiant's smile was weak. She obviously figured this was a lost cause, but Harri still planned to follow through. Even if she did want to inflict a little payback for how Mother Defiant treated her firm's newest partner.

They both rose from their chairs, and Harri escorted Mother Defiant to the front doors.

After the final good-bye with the superhero and she left, Harri walked back into the reception area, the original foyer of the Lechuza Building. She was still impressed how good their building manager Miguel Esperanza made the original Art Deco design look when his team renovated the place.

As she passed the reception desk, their assistant Patty Ames winced and put a call on hold. "Harri, your ex-husband in on line 1."

Now, why the hell was Eddie calling her? The new Mrs. Lewis had thrown a major hissy fit about him talking to Harri. It didn't matter that things were long over between them, or how much Eddie adored

Sarah and their two kids. She was one insecure woman. Therefore, if Eddie was calling, it was business-related.

"Thanks, Patty."

Harri strode into her office and sat down to compose herself before she picked up the receiver on her phone set and jabbed the button next to the blinking light. "Hey, Eddie! Does Sarah know you're off the leash?"

So much for any composure.

"Not funny, Harri," he snapped. "This is business." Of course.

"And what can I do for Canyon Pointe's FBI office today?" she teased as she leaned back in her chair.

"Have you spoken to Miss Purrception lately?" Eddie said.

"Not since last month," Harri answered. "We're still fighting the extraditions to France and Brazil. Why?"

"Are you sure?" Eddie sounded more tense than usually.

"Eddie, out of all our marital problems, I've never out-and-out lied to you," Harri said. "Either spit out why you called, or hang up."

"Miss Purrception escaped from Mauvaises Prison last night."

"What!" Harri bolted upright.

"It gets better," Eddie added. "Byron Trubble escaped with her."

Harri's heart lodged in her throat. Retired general Byron S. Trubble. Former head of the secret black ops organization known as Corvus.

And the one person who wanted Harri dead more than any other supervillain in the world.

Hero In Camera is currently available for preorder at your favorite retailers!

Acknowledgements

As usual, much love and gratitude go to my cover artist Elaina Lee and my formatter Jaye Manus.

And lots of hugs and kisses to my Darling Husband, who picked up a lot of take-out while I struggled to finish this book in the midst of a worldwide pandemic and massive protests against police brutality across the United States and other countries. Justice is something everyone deserves.